CW01626699

PATRIOT FORCE

(A Zack Force Action Thriller—Book 1)

VIN STRONG

Vin Strong

Vin Strong is the author of the BRIANNA DAGGER spy thriller series, comprising five books (and counting), and of the ZACK FORCE thriller series, comprising five books (and counting).

An avid reader and lifelong fan of the thriller genres, Vin loves to hear from you, so please feel free to visit vinstrongauthor.com to learn more and stay in touch.

ISBN: 978-1-0943-9704-7

BOOKS BY VIN STRONG

ZACK FORCE THRILLER SERIES
PATRIOT FORCE (Book #1)
PATRIOT DOWN (Book #2)
PATRIOT RISING (Book #3)
PATRIOT STRIKE (Book #4)
PATRIOT TARGET (Book #5)

BRIANNA DAGGER THRILLER SERIES
MAZE OF SPIES (Book #1)
MAZE OF TRAITORS (Book #2)
MAZE OF LIES (Book #3)
MAZE OF SHADOWS (Book #4)
MAZE OF SECRETS (Book #5)

PROLOGUE

Kim Rhee adjusted the weight of his tool belt as he strode through the cavernous turbine hall, his movements mirroring those of the other maintenance workers clocking in for their shift. Park Ji-hoon walked a few paces behind him, both men wearing the same blue overalls and hard hats that were standard issue at the Montrose Nuclear Power Plant. Their faces, scrubbed clean of any distinguishing marks or blemishes, were as nondescript as the gray concrete walls surrounding them.

"Another day, another dollar, huh?" Park remarked casually, though his eyes constantly scanned their surroundings.

"Keep your voice down," Kim muttered without turning his head. "Remember, we're just a couple of regular joes here to fix pipes."

Kim knew they had to maintain a low profile. Every worker was just another cog in the machine, easily replaceable, easily forgotten. That anonymity was their greatest asset. Their features—Park's slight build and Kim's average height—blended seamlessly into the sea of employees. It was as if the plant itself had absorbed them, two more shadows among the many that flickered in the fluorescent light.

He felt the familiar weight of the hidden device against his chest, concealed beneath the fabric of his jumpsuit. It was no larger than a pack of cards, but its potential for destruction was immeasurable.

His heart rate quickened at the thought of what lay ahead, but he schooled his features into an expression of bored indifference. They couldn't afford to attract attention, not when they were so close.

"Here," Park murmured, pausing beside an inconspicuous panel labeled 'Electrical Access – Authorized Personnel Only.' They were alone, the distant hum of machinery and muted conversations among workers fading behind them.

Kim nodded, his pulse quickening as he glanced around to ensure they remained unobserved. He slipped out the device, its matte black casing designed to be as unremarkable as the tools they carried. With practiced ease, he opened the panel, revealing a tangle of wires and circuits.

"Make it quick," Kim said, keeping one eye on the corridor. Park worked deftly, attaching the device to the plant's wiring with a set of miniature clamps. It was silent, emitting no light or signal that would betray its activation.

"Done," Park said, closing the panel with a soft click. They exchanged a terse nod, the magnitude of their actions hanging between them, unspoken but deeply felt.

"Let's move," Kim said, stepping away from the wall. As they retraced their steps, the tiny red LED on the device blinked once, twice, then steadied—a harbinger of the chaos to come.

They had barely rounded the next corner when the first alarm sounded, shrill and piercing against the industrial cacophony. Red lights pulsed overhead, casting an ominous glow across the plant workers' faces, now etched with confusion and growing fear.

"What the hell is that?" someone shouted, their voice lost in the sudden eruption of activity as technicians scrambled toward control panels, flipping through manuals and barking orders.

"System malfunction!" another yelled. "We've got multiple warnings! Coolant loss, reactor pressure rising!"

Park kept his head down, mirroring the panic around him, while Kim's heart raced. This was the moment of truth, the fulcrum upon which their entire operation pivoted. Every second counted, every reaction a variable in their meticulously crafted equation.

"Evacuation protocol!" came the command, authoritative and urgent, over the plant's intercom system. Workers began to pour from every doorway, a flood of bodies moving with single-minded intent toward the exits.

Yet amidst the pandemonium, Kim remained acutely aware of the surveillance cameras dotting the ceiling, the eyes that could unravel everything. He adjusted his cap lower, face angled away from their gaze, and moved with the crowd, his and Park's anonymity their greatest asset as the symphony of alarms crescendoed into anarchy.

This was their design, the invisible hand guiding events toward an inevitable conclusion, each step away from the epicenter a silent testament to their resolve. The power plant, once a bastion of energy and life, was now teetering on the brink, a victim to unseen forces that lurked within its very walls.

"Is it done?" Park whispered sharply, his voice barely rising above the cacophony of alarms and screams that filled the air.

Kim Rhee nodded, a grim smile twisting his lips. They were shoulder to shoulder in the throng of employees, but their calm was an island in the storm. "It's done," he said, his voice tinged with satisfaction. "The great serpent has been fed its own venom."

"Long live the Republic," Park murmured under his breath.

"May our sacrifices be the dawn of a new era," Kim replied, his gaze fixed on a future only they could see. The chaos around them was merely the first ripple of a wave that would wash across nations.

"Remember, brother," Park said, jostling against Kim as they moved with the panicked crowd, "our faces are those of ghosts here. We fade into the night, and our deeds become legend."

Kim knew the truth of these words as intimately as the plans etched into his mind. They had trained for this moment, their identities nothing more than smokescreens. Beneath the nondescript uniforms, they were the harbingers of change, the unseen hand that would shake empires.

Through the bedlam, Kim remained vigilant, acutely aware of every glance that skimmed past him, every step that brought him closer to escape. He adjusted the ID badge hanging from his neck, ensuring it sat askew, unidentifiable in the blur of movement. It was all about blending in, becoming part of the chaos while keeping a razor-sharp focus on the path ahead.

As they approached the exit, the steel doors loomed like the gates to freedom, but Kim kept his emotions in check. There would be time for relief when they were miles away, submerged in the depths of anonymity once again. For now, each breath was measured, each step calculated, as they edged toward salvation.

When we walk out these doors, we are no longer the hands that lit the fuse, Kim thought. *We are simply shadows, fading back into obscurity.*

Outside, the sky was painted with the colors of apocalypse—orange and crimson hues that bled together as if the heavens themselves were ablaze. The nuclear plant, once a monument to human ingenuity, now stood as a crumbling testament to its hubris, the meltdown in full swing. Concrete walls, designed to withstand nature's worst tantrums, cracked and groaned under the pressure of their own betrayal.

Kim watched as billows of thick, acrid smoke clawed their way into the atmosphere, the smell of scorched metal and panic tainting the air. The sirens continued their relentless wail, a death knell for the innocence that had perished alongside the plant's integrity.

"Look at them," Park murmured, nodding toward the remaining employees who scrambled like ants beneath a magnifying glass. They were fighting a losing battle against the monstrous energy that threatened to consume everything in its insatiable maw.

Desperation, Kim thought, observing the scene with a detachment that bordered on the clinical. This was the result of their actions—the chaos they had sown with such precision. Yet, there was no guilt in Kim's heart, only the cold certainty that they had done what was necessary for their greater purpose.

"Let's go," he said, pulling his gaze away from the destruction. They needed to disappear into the night, to become phantoms once more in a world that might never understand their sacrifice.

As they moved away from the dying behemoth, Kim couldn't help but glance back. The inferno reflected in his eyes, a mirror to the fire that burned within him—a fire fueled by years of training and indoctrination, by the belief that his actions served a cause far greater than any individual life.

"History will remember us," Park whispered, his voice heavy with a mixture of pride and something darker, unspoken.

"History will remember nothing of us," Kim corrected quietly. "And that is how it must be."

Their footsteps were lost in the chaos, two silent figures retreating into the anonymity of the dark. Behind them, the power plant continued its descent into ruin, a dying giant whose roars faded into the stillness of the night.

This is just the beginning, Kim thought. *And if the rest of our plans unfold so easily...we will soon have this country at its knees.*

CHAPTER ONE

Zack Force's fists slammed into the leather-wrapped punching bag, the sound filling the spacious, dim interior of the old barn he had renovated into his own makeshift gym. Hanging chains flickered with patches of rust under the weak lamps' light as they swayed in response to his vigorous assault. The smell of old hay and damp earth, combined with the familiar tang of sweat and leather, brought back memories of his upbringing in rural Alabama.

His muscles ached, begging for rest, but he forced himself to keep going. He couldn't slack, couldn't take it easy on himself. His country's safety depended on him, and though he was realistic enough to understand he was only one piece on a massive board, he didn't believe in half-measures. The blood of a patriot ran in his veins, burning with an intensity that had been ignited by the loss of his father.

Zack pummeled the bag with a right hook, remembering Douglas Force, standing tall in his military uniform, squared shoulders carrying the weight of duty effortlessly. His father's intense gaze had always reflected the unwavering commitment to his country, an attitude that Zack had inherited and cherished.

Pausing for a moment, Zack stripped off his sweat-soaked shirt, revealing a roadmap of scars that criss-crossed over his chiseled torso. Each one was a reminder of a mission completed, a danger subdued, a life saved.

Or sometimes, a life lost.

He traced a particularly gnarly one that coiled around his side like a python, the result of an encounter with a terrorist's knife during his early years with the Department of National Security, a new agency formed to combat the rising tide of domestic terrorism. The pain had been excruciating, but Zack remembered pushing through it, determined to carry out his mission. It was what Douglas would have done, and Zack would be damned if he'd do any less.

Zack swiped a towel from a nearby chair, wiping away the beads of sweat cascading down his face and chest. With every drawn breath, he could taste the years of dedication and hard work, the salty tang of sacrifice. His muscles gave an approving hum as he walked toward the corner of the makeshift gym where an old vinyl record player sat on a wooden crate. Beside it lay a small collection of worn-out records that had once belonged to his father.

He picked one out at random, not needing to look at the faded label to know it was his father's favorite – a collection of old country ballads that had served as the soundtrack of his childhood. With careful fingers, he placed the needle down into the grooves of the vinyl record and let the twangy guitar notes fill the air, wrapping around him like a comforting cloak.

The music tugged at the corners of his heart, stirring memories and emotions too deep for words. Zack stared out through a narrow window, into the impenetrable darkness outside where only the faint outlines of age-old trees were visible. As he listened to the haunting melodies, he was transported back to a simpler time when life was about hay fields and creek swims, not terrorists and covert operations.

Zack's grip tightened around the worn towel, memories flooding back with such force that it felt like a sucker punch to his gut. He saw his mother dancing around the kitchen, her laughter harmonizing with the sweet melodies; he remembered Sunday drives in their ancient pickup, his dad singing along to these very songs on the crackling radio.

Zack's heart pounded rhythmically to the nostalgic tune, conjuring up the smell of his mother's apple pie baking in the oven, the hearty laughter of his father echoing through their old Alabama homestead. Zack closed his eyes, allowing himself to bask in the warmth of those long-ago days.

One of these days, Dad, he thought, *I'm going to avenge you. One of these days, those terrorists are going to pay.*

* * *

Zack was all business by the time he pulled up to the headquarters of the Department of National Security. He turned into the parking lot, pausing to show the security guard his badge before driving through. He parked in the same spot he'd parked in since joining the department seven years ago. He got out of the car, locked it with a click of a button, and strode toward the flight up steps leading up into the heart of the building.

Once inside the glass and concrete monolith, he strode through the security checkpoint with a nod to the guards. The cold sterility of the place never quite reached him. Instead, he found comfort in the unchanging environment—a stark contrast to the chaos he often faced beyond these walls. He made his way down the long corridor, the rhythmic click of his shoes on the polished floor echoing like the ticking of some great clock measuring the beats of his life.

"Force," called a familiar voice, tinged with the slightest hint of a New York twang. "You planning to take down terrorists with that scowl, or are you saving it just for me?"

Zack's lips curled into an involuntary smile as he turned to face his partner, Riley Carter. She leaned against the doorframe of their shared office, her arms crossed and her eyebrow raised in playful challenge. Her sharp eyes missed nothing—never had.

"Riley," Zack said, the tightness in his chest easing at the sight of her. "If my scowl could take down terrorists, we'd both be out of a job."

"Then it's a good thing I know how to make you crack a smile," she quipped, pushing away from the doorframe. There was a grace to her movements that belied her toughness, a remnant of her past life on the streets of New York.

Zack and Riley had many similarities: They were both workaholics, both dedicated to their country, both determined to stop at nothing in their pursuit of justice. While Zack relied on analytics, however, Riley tended to take a more human approach, seeking out relationships and building empathy with victims. This difference in their approaches often caused them to clash with one another.

Together, they entered the cramped confines of their office, a space cluttered with monitors and strewn papers—the remnants of cases both old and new. They settled into the well-worn chairs that faced each other across a desk littered with case files and takeaway coffee cups, the detritus of too many late nights.

"Alright, let's dive in," Zack said, flipping open a manila folder. "We've got leads on the smuggling ring out of Norfolk."

Carter nodded, pulling her own stack of color-coded folders from the side drawer of the desk. Years of working together had turned their routine into a masterful ballet of sorts—a harmony of movements performed without need for words. Just a glance exchanged between them was enough to set the wheels in motion.

Opening one of the red-marked folders, Riley scanned the first few lines, her olive-green eyes flickering with unspoken thoughts and questions. "Looks like we've got another shipment due in two days," she said, her voice a low murmur in the otherwise silent room.

"We need to catch them red-handed this time," Zack said, his jaw set in a hard line. "We've been chasing these guys for months. It's time we put an end to it."

"I'll reach out to my CI," Riley said. "If we offer him and his family protection—"

Before Riley could finish, Zack's phone erupted with a frantic symphony of vibrations. Zack glanced at the caller ID: his boss, Director Elizabeth “Liz” Murdock. She had worked closely with Zack's father during her early years as an agent, which created a strange dynamic between her and Zack, both professional and personal.

"Force," he answered, always expecting the worst.

"You with Carter?" Liz asked without preamble.

Zack met Riley's gaze. "That's right."

"Good. There's been an incident in Pennsylvania, and I need you both out there."

"What about the Norfolk case? We're getting close to—"

"I'll hand that off to someone else," Liz cut in. "This is top priority."

Zack paused, wondering just how bad it might be. "Dare I ask what happened?"

"It's the Montrose Nuclear Power Plant. There's been a meltdown."

The silence in the office became a vacuum, sucking away any semblance of normalcy they had known moments before. The morning sun, gleaming through the blinds, cast shadows that seemed to darken with the news, turning the room into a chiaroscuro painting of impending doom.

"Evacuations are underway," Liz continued with a troubled sigh, "but we need you and Carter there, now. This isn't just a disaster—it could be an attack. And if it is an attack…" She paused, taking a deep breath. "I'm worried it could be just the beginning of a larger plan."

CHAPTER TWO

Zack's boots crunched on a mosaic of shattered glass and debris as he and Riley stepped into the shadow of Pennsylvania's Montrose Nuclear Power Plant. The air was thick with acrid smoke, a stark contrast to the clean, fresh air of his Alabama childhood. Sirens and shouts filled the air as emergency personnel moved about, searching for survivors in the wreckage of last night's meltdown.

Both Zack and Riley were dressed in radiation suits, their bodies encapsulated in layers of lead-lined fabric, their faces hidden behind fogged-up visors. Their movements were sluggish, encumbered by the weight of protective gear.

"Agent Force? Agent Carter?" A harried official, dressed in a similar suit and with a Geiger counter in his hand, approached them. "I'm Director Hammond. Thank God you're here."

"Director." Zack offered a curt nod. "Brief us."

Hammond took a shaky breath. "It's...hellish. The core overheated, containment systems failed. Explosion. We managed to shut down the reactor, but the damage is extensive. Radiation levels are uncertain. It's a miracle the death toll isn't higher."

"Any idea what caused the failure?"

"Mechanical failure," Hammond began, "is the official stance, but..." He trailed off, glancing around nervously, lowering his voice. "There have been whispers. Discrepancies in the logs, unusual malfunctions weeks prior. I don't want to cause a panic, but..."

"But we're not ruling out sabotage," Zack finished for him, his jaw tightening at the implication.

"Exactly," Hammond said, relief evident in his eyes that the agents understood the gravity of the situation.

Riley stepped forward, her tone compassionate yet firm. "We'll need access to everything: records, security footage, personnel files. And your full cooperation."

"Of course, anything," Hammond agreed, already motioning for an aide to assist them.

"How close can we get?" Zack asked. "With the radiation, I mean."

Hammond bit his lip, taking a moment to consider. "It's difficult to say at the moment. We're getting wildly different reports on radiation levels. This is no Chernobyl, but there could still be pockets of radiation in high concentrations, so your best bet is to keep checking the levels yourself. Here, take my counter." He handed Zack his Geiger counter.

"Thank you," Zack said. "We'll head closer, see if we can find anyone who saw what happened."

Hammond nodded. "Good luck. And if you start to feel sick...run like hell."

The two agents nodded their affirmation and walked deeper into the smoky abyss of the plant wreckage. Each step Zack took sounded a hollow echo in his ears, a stark reminder of the disaster that had occurred here. He moved carefully, the Geiger counter flickering erratically, its readings bobbing between safe and hazardous.

Zack found himself holding his breath every time the needle erred toward the red zone. He'd read about radiation poisoning, seen pictures of what it could do to human tissue, but standing here, knowing he was walking through an invisible minefield that could kill him from the inside out, made it disturbingly real.

"Zack, over here!" Riley's voice cut through Zack's thoughts. He turned, following her pointed gesture to where a company employee sat on the curb, his face ashen, eyes wide with shock. He wasn't wearing a suit, which suggested he may have only recently escaped the plant.

Without a word, Zack strode over, his mind already forming the questions he needed answers to. "Tell me everything you saw," he demanded.

The man flinched, recoiling from Zack's intensity. "Uh...I... It was just so fast," the man stuttered. Zack's impatience simmered below the surface, but he kept his expression neutral. Time was of the essence, and this man could hold the key to what they were dealing with.

"We need to get him away from the plant," Riley said. "It's too dangerous."

"The radiation levels are low here," Zack answered. He turned his attention back to the man. "Focus. We need details."

The man, however, seemed to fold inward, his words trapped behind a barrier of trauma as he stared into the distance with hollow eyes.

"Zack," Riley said sharply. "He's in danger. This isn't the place to question him."

"Our country may be in danger," Zack answered. "I just need a few answers. Now, are you going to help me or what?"

Clenching her jaw in frustration, Riley knelt beside the shaken worker, her hand lightly touching his arm. "Hey, it's okay. We're here to help. Can you tell me your name?" Her voice was soft, a stark contrast to Zack's commanding tone. The man's breathing slowed, visibly calmed by her empathetic approach.

"Tom...Tom Sanders. I work in the control room," he managed, glancing up at Riley with tentative trust.

"Tom, can you walk us through what happened?"

"Everything was normal until...until it wasn't." Tom's eyes glazed over as he recounted the events leading up to the meltdown. "Alarms started blaring, systems shutting down. We tried to stabilize the reactor, but it was like someone...someone else was in control."

"Someone else?" Riley asked.

"I don't know how to explain it. Procedures we've done a hundred times, suddenly none of it worked. It's like...like they knew exactly how to hit us where it hurt."

"Thank you, Tom. You did good," Riley said, giving his arm a reassuring squeeze. "Now let's get you away from the plant." She shot Zack a glance, as if to make it clear she didn't like the way he'd handled that.

As Riley led Tom away, Zack's eyes scanned the ruins, taking in the charred and twisted metal that had once stood as a testament to human engineering. The sight was apocalyptic; blackened structures jutted out at odd angles, and the air was thick with the acrid stench of burnt insulation and fear.

Following his gut, Zack approached the charred remains of what was once the heart of the plant. He felt a shudder crawl up his spine as he ducked under a dangerously leaning beam, wincing as a sooty residue transferred onto his hand. He could almost hear the groan of the wreckage that was once a marvel of modern technology.

he pushed farther into the ruins, his every sense alert for any residual danger hidden within the rubble. The Geiger counter buzzed incessantly in his grip, the numbers on its screen bouncing erratically. He thought of all the training he'd received on radiation, and he mentally calculated how much he was exposing himself to—and how long he could do so before the effects would be irreversible.

I need to know what happened here, he thought. *I can't leave until I do.*

Every instinct he had was screaming that this was deliberate, a carefully orchestrated dance of death and destruction. And if that was the case, then every second they spent not catching the perpetrator brought them closer to another potential disaster. And Zack Force did not let threats to his country go unchallenged—not while he still drew breath.

He whirled at the sound of footsteps behind him. It was Riley, her suit smeared with soot and her eyes hard with determination. She was holding a radiation meter in one hand and a camera in the other.

"Good," Zack said. "We need to document everything—then we can look over it later, if necessary." Every snapped wire, every out-of-place bolt was now a clue, a silent witness to the calamity that had unfolded.

If Riley was still bothered by what had happened earlier, she didn't show it. Zack was grateful—they needed to focus on searching the ruins.

They continued forward, picking their way through the labyrinth of destruction. The twisted metal and rubble beneath their feet seemed to groan with the weight of the disaster's aftermath.

"Zack," Riley said as their Geiger counters began to beep more feverishly, "the radiation levels are too high. We've already exposed ourselves too much."

"We need to know what happened," Zack said. "You can go back—I'll be there in a few minutes."

"No." Riley's refusal was firm, unyielding. "We're partners, Zack. I'm not leaving you."

"That's your choice."

She stepped in front of him. "And I'm not letting you make a fatal mistake, either."

As much as Zack wanted to argue, he knew Riley was right. The radiation levels were getting dangerous, and staying longer would only risk their lives further. But his pride fought against his logic; his desire to get to the bottom of what happened here was like a siren call that he was struggling to resist.

"You know you're more stubborn than a mule, don't you?" he asked.

She shrugged. "Takes one to know one."

He grunted and turned around. Together, they made their way out of the ruins, each step away from the heart of the disaster feeling to Zack like a defeat. The Geiger counters slowly quieted, their urgency fading as the danger lessened.

"Someone must have seen something," Zack murmured. "We need to interview everyone, try to piece together what happened."

"Think it was an inside job?" Riley asked.

"It's hard to imagine otherwise. Just infiltrating security would be a nightmare, but if you're already on the payroll and can come and go as you please?"

The conversation was interrupted by Director Hammond, who approached them alongside a woman in a crisp white lab coat, her red hair pulled back tightly away from her face. "Agents Force and Carter," Hammond said, "I'd like you to meet Dr. Eleanor Brixton. She's our resident nuclear physicist. She has some...*theories* on what happened here." The tone of Hammond's voice suggested that what they were about to hear would not be good news.

Zack and Riley shook hands with Dr. Brixton, who gave them a firm, tight smile. "I've been looking at the preliminary data and speaking with employees," she said. "This wasn't any ordinary meltdown—there's no simple mechanical failure or operator error that could have caused this."

"Are you saying it was sabotage?" Zack asked.

Dr. Brixton nodded. "I can almost guarantee it."

"How do you know?" Riley asked.

"Someone overrode the safety controls," the doctor said. "A plant like this is designed so that such a thing is impossible, at least without a whole team of engineers being in on the plot, which is highly unlikely. But despite all the safeguards in place, someone found a way to manipulate the reactor and trigger a meltdown."

"How?" Zack asked. "How did they override the safety controls?"

Dr. Brixton pressed her lips together. "I can't say for sure...but my guess is they hacked into the system, perhaps by using a device with a set of preprogrammed commands. That's the only way everything could happen so fast."

"Sounds sophisticated," Zack murmured.

Dr. Brixton nodded. "Very sophisticated. This wasn't done by some disgruntled employee. Whoever was involved, they were professionals: highly skilled, highly trained. They knew the plant, and they knew how to cause the most damage."

Zack and Riley exchanged a glance. This was worse than they had thought.

"We need to find who's behind this immediately," Zack said, his jaw tightening. "The person — or people — we're dealing with are not just a threat to this facility...they're a threat to national security."

"And potentially more than that," Dr. Brixton added. "This power plant has sister facilities worldwide. If someone has figured out how to bypass the safeguards here—"

"Then the same methods could be used elsewhere," Riley said.

CHAPTER THREE

The interior of the makeshift field office was cramped but organized, with maps and screens adorning every possible space. Zack's eyes swept over the room, taking in the information overload.

This'll have to do, he thought.

He moved toward a table strewn with incident reports and transcripts, his movements deliberate, like a predator zoning in on prey. He picked up a stack of papers, the pages crisp against his calloused fingers. Every fiber of his being was focused on finding those responsible for the attack on the plant, no matter the cost.

"Let's start with the interviews with employees, see if anyone noticed any unusual behavior leading up to the meltdown," Zack said, handing a portion of the documents to Riley.

"Got it," Riley said, already engrossed in a transcript. Her brow furrowed as she read, her ability to empathize with the witnesses evident in the way she absorbed their recounted terror.

Zack sifted through the reports, each one a window into the horrors of the night before. Voices echoed in his head, snippets of frantic calls and screams that haunted the edges of his thoughts. It wasn't just about justice; it was personal. Someone had dared to threaten his country, the very thing his father died defending.

The witness statements were all over the place, filled with panic and disjointed accounts, many of them contradicting one another—or even themselves. Were these harmless mistakes the product of a chaotic and panic-inducing event, or could some of these be deliberate lies intended to divert suspicion from the attackers?

"We could have a team of twenty people going through these," Riley said, "and it would still take all day."

Zack didn't answer. He was thinking about the very-real possibility that this was an inside job. How long had the terrorists planned this? How many times had they entered the plant, scoping it out and meticulously detailing every aspect of their deadly sabotage?

"Where were the security cameras?" he asked aloud, breaking the silence that hung thick in the room.

"They were disabled," Riley replied, her voice heavy. "Some were destroyed outright in the blast, while others were so obscured by smoke and debris as to render them useless."

"Any unusual maintenance checks or private contractors on-site in the days leading to the attack?"

Riley shook her head. "Not that I'm aware of."

Just then, Zack's phone vibrated sharply against the metal desk, jolting him from his thoughts.

"Who is it?" Riley asked without looking up from her own stack of papers.

"Unknown number," Zack murmured, thumbing the device to life. The message was as cryptic as it was unsettling. Zack read it aloud: "'Check out Galen Fisher—fired from Montrose last year. Not happy about it.'"

Riley sat up straighter. "Sounds like we have our first lead."

"Or our first wild goose chase," Zack said. "This could just be a personal vendetta."

"You really can't take good news, can you?"

He grunted. "Let's see who our mystery texter is."

Turning to the laptop at his elbow, he attempted to trace the number, fingers flying over the screen in practiced movements. But it only led him to a discarded burner phone. Someone had been very careful.

"Damn it," he muttered under his breath. "Someone sure doesn't want to get wrapped up in this any more than they already are."

"Let me take a crack at Galen Fisher," Riley said, pulling up a new window on her laptop. Her fingers danced across the keyboard, the clicks punctuating the tense silence. She let out a low whistle. "Here we go. Looks like Fisher made some serious threats to plant management after his termination. Said he'd 'make them regret it.'"

"Why was he fired in the first place?" Zack asked.

"Looks like a series of infractions: tardiness, insubordination, neglect of duties," Riley said after a moment of scrolling through Fisher's file. "According to his supervisor's notes, Fisher was often spotted in off-limit areas, claiming he had lost his way."

"Or looking for vulnerabilities in the system?" Zack suggested, his brow creased with thought.

"Possibly," Riley conceded. "And according to this, he was involved in an accident on site about three years ago. A pipe burst, and he sustained severe burns. He couldn't work for six months."

"So we've got motive—both personal and professional," Zack said. "But would he have the means to pull this off?"

Zack turned back to his own workstation, driven by a need to piece together the puzzle before them. A quick search for Galen Fisher brought up more than just a disgruntled ex-employee. Connections to a notorious criminal gang surfaced, drawing a line between petty revenge and organized terror.

"Riley," he said, his voice tight, "it looks like Fisher's tied in with the Black Serpents."

Her head snapped up, eyes widening. "The drug runners?"

"More like drug-running, gun-smuggling, do-anything-for-the-right-price kind of guys. The Feds have had him on their watchlist for the past six months, but there's nothing official—no arrests involving the Black Serpents, nothing that would cause him to fail a background check. Still, there's no telling how long he's been involved with them."

"Shit." Riley's face hardened. "That elevates things from personal vendetta to potential national threat."

"Exactly." Zack leaned back in his chair, the weight of the situation settling on his shoulders. If Fisher was secretly working with the Black Serpents, then the attack on the nuclear plant could be just the beginning, as Liz had feared.

"Are we sure he was even here last night?" he asked.

"Well, I'd say we could check the security footage, but..."

Zack tapped his fingers thoughtfully on the desk. "Some of the perimeter cameras looked okay," he said. "They might be able to tell us who entered the building for that particular shift. It's a lot of people, but if we're only looking for one person, it's doable."

Zack's fingers danced across the keyboard with practiced ease, pulling up multiple screens of security footage. Riley rose and stood behind him, peering over his shoulder.

Zack studied the dozens of workers entering the plant for last night's shift. As he scrolled through the footage, Riley suddenly spoke up.

"Stop there," she said.

Zack paused the video. Riley pointed at a figure on the screen, and Zack zoomed in to get a better look.

"That's Fisher," Riley murmured from behind him.

The man in the video had his cap pulled low, obstructing his face from view. But the distinctive scar down his left arm, marking his earlier accident on site, was undeniable.

"Looks like he was on-site at the time of the attack," Zack said, a fierce satisfaction kindling within him. "The question is, how'd he get in? Did he steal a badge?"

"Or maybe someone on the inside helped him," Riley suggested.

"Either way, he illegally entered the building shortly after the attack. We need to find him."

"His termination record mentioned threats against management," Riley recalled, folding her arms. "But jumping from angry ex-employee to terrorist is a leap. Why take it?"

"Power," Zack answered, his gaze not leaving the frozen image of Fisher. "Control. Revenge. Take your pick. They all lead to the same dark place."

"Or money," Riley suggested. "Maybe the Black Serpents promised him a pay-out or a position within their ranks."

"Could be," Zack conceded, rubbing his chin thoughtfully. "But the Black Serpents aren't known for playing well with outsiders. If they brought Fisher in, it's because he has something they want."

"Skills? Access?" Riley asked, her brows knitting in concentration.

"Both," Zack surmised. "He knows the plant inside and out. He could make the attack look like an accident. Cover their tracks."

"Which would give them time to plan their next move without anyone breathing down their necks," Riley finished.

"Exactly." Zack's jaw clenched. The implications were chilling. Fisher's fall from loyal employee to vengeful saboteur was a story as old as time, but with the Black Serpents in the mix, it was a powder keg waiting to ignite.

"Whatever the gang's planning, it's big," Zack said, his voice low. "And if Fisher's our way in, we need to grab him before he disappears into their world completely."

"Agreed," Riley said. "I'll go see if I can track down his address."

As Riley searched for Fisher's address, Zack stared at the screen, studying the man in the baseball cap. *What's your plan?* he wondered. *And how are the Black Serpents involved in all this?*

"Damn it," Riley muttered, frustration creeping into her voice as she hit the backspace key with more force than necessary. "He's a ghost. No current address, no recent utilities or cell phone contracts. It's like he knew we'd be looking and wiped his slate clean."

Zack's fingers drummed on the desk, a rhythmic tapping that betrayed his own impatience. He pulled out his phone. "Maybe Neil can help us."

He placed the call, bringing the phone to his ear.

"Neil, it's Zack. We've got a situation."

"A situation?" Neil repeated with a note of amused interest. "Sounds fun"

"It isn't. There's a man named Galen Fisher, worked at the Montrose Nuclear Power Plant until two years ago. I need an address, any known associates' places, hideouts—anything you can scrape up fast."

"Give me five," came the tech expert's confident reply, a hint of excitement lacing his tone. That was Neil—always relishing a challenge. Zack could picture him, eyes alight behind the glow of his monitors, fingers dancing across the keyboard.

"Five minutes," Zack repeated, glancing at Riley, who nodded in silent understanding. He hung up, pocketing the phone.

As they waited, Zack paced the length of their cramped space, the tick-tock of the wall clock mocking their urgency. He replayed everything they knew about Fisher, trying to anticipate his next move. The Black Serpents were not amateurs; they'd cover their tracks, protect their own. Fisher was their loose end, their vulnerability, and Zack knew there was a good chance that if the Serpents realized Fisher was under suspicion, they would make him disappear.

Permanently.

The phone buzzed against his thigh, breaking his train of thought. Zack snatched it up, seeing Neil's name flash on the screen.

"Got something," Neil said. "Fisher's been using a burner, but he slipped up. Made a call from a landline out in rural Pennsylvania. Small place, off the grid. Coordinates coming your way."

"Good work," Zack replied, though the words felt inadequate for the surge of adrenaline that Neil's news sent coursing through him. Rural Pennsylvania—it fit Fisher's MO. Remote, isolated, a place where a man could disappear. But not from Zack Force.

Zack ended the call. "Riley," he said, his voice low but urgent as he turned to his partner, "if Neil's right, Fisher's holed up with the Black Serpents. They know how to play dirty, and they won't give him up without a fight."

Riley nodded grimly, her eyes sharp and focused. Her fingers danced over her own set of gear—a bulletproof vest she strapped on with practiced ease. "Then we'll be ready for them. What's our play?"

"Stealth is our best bet," Zack replied, slipping extra magazines into his belt. "We need to approach the hideout under the radar. Once we make contact, we'll have to adapt quickly."

"Agreed," Riley said as she checked her weapons. "We have the element of surprise, at least. Let's not waste it."

Zack felt a familiar tension coiling in his muscles, the adrenaline already beginning to pump through his veins. He pulled on his tactical gloves, each movement deliberate, honed by years of training and real-world operations that had etched themselves into his muscle memory. Every action was a silent promise – to himself, to Riley, to his father – that he would protect what mattered most.

"We have to take him alive, Zack," Riley said. "Whether he's guilty or not—we need to be able to question him."

"I know. Why do you feel the need to tell me?"

"Sometimes you seem to think you're living in the Wild West. That's all."

Zack wasn't sure whether to take this as a compliment or an insult. "I'll keep that in mind," he said.

"Good. Because if we don't get the opportunity to question him, we might lose our only chance at figuring out why this attack happened—and what might be next."

CHAPTER FOUR

Zack lay prone on the cold, damp ground, peering through the binoculars at the dilapidated warehouse that served as Galen Fisher's hideout. The structure stood isolated amidst a graveyard of rusted machinery and overgrown weeds—a perfect haunt for those who preferred shadows to sunlight.

"Four...no, five sentries," Zack murmured as he scanned the perimeter. "Two by the front entrance, one on the roof. The other two are patrolling."

Riley, positioned beside him, mirrored his actions as she gazed through another pair of binoculars. "Black Serpents' jackets," she said. "Not good."

The Black Serpents were notorious for their ruthlessness. If they had taken Fisher under their wing, it meant trouble. Zack pictured the distinctive gang insignia – the coiled serpent ready to strike – and felt a familiar surge of adrenaline. They couldn't afford a shootout. Fisher might be the key to unlocking the mystery behind the Montrose Nuclear Power Plant sabotage, but if the Black Serpents realized Fisher's value to the Department of National Security, they'd put a bullet in him before allowing his capture.

"If we spook them, Fisher's dead," Zack said quietly, his jaw tightening. "We need to extract him silently."

"Agreed." Riley paused, considering their options. "Back door. It's less guarded, and there's enough cover from these woods to get us close unnoticed. We'll need to take out the sentry quietly, though."

"Right." Zack nodded, his mind conjuring up the tactical training embedded deep within him. Stealth was paramount—every movement would have to be measured, every decision precise. "We go in silent, no shots unless absolutely necessary. Hand-to-hand takedowns only. Can't risk an alarm."

Riley's eyes met his, and he saw the same steely resolve that had made her such a formidable partner. She understood the gravity of the situation just as well as he did.

"Once inside, we stick together until we find Fisher. Then we reassess." Zack paused, visualizing the layout of the warehouse from the blueprints they had studied earlier. "Remember, he's got that burn scar down his left arm. Should make him easier to ID."

"Got it," Riley said with a curt nod. "And Zack..."

He turned to face her, noting the concern in her eyes. "Yeah?"

"No need to be a hero, okay?"

He knew she was thinking of the power plant, and how he'd wanted to press on into the ruins, despite the radiation.

"I'm not planning to get shot, if that's what you mean," he said.

"Good." She smiled. "Then let's avoid getting shot together."

With that, the two agents rose from their hiding places and stole forward like ghosts, slipping from tree to tree.

"Twenty meters to the back entrance," Zack whispered. He could almost feel his father's presence beside him, guiding him, strengthening his resolve. He hoped his father was proud of the man he'd become.

"Copy," Riley replied, her eyes scanning the trees for any sign of movement. "I don't like this silence."

"Neither do I," Zack admitted, his gut tensing with a mix of anticipation and dread. Every step felt like a dance with danger, one misstep away from disaster.

They paused at the edge of the building, pressing themselves flat against the cool metal siding. Zack peered around the corner, noting the absence of guards at the door. It was either a stroke of luck or a trap. He chose to believe the former, trusting in the prep work they had done, in the unwavering sharpness of his senses honed by years of training.

He moved around the corner and, once Riley was in position beside him, he tested the handle. Locked, but not an obstacle for someone with Zack's expertise. A slim pick slipped from his sleeve, and within seconds, the lock gave way with a soft click. They entered the building, Zack leading.

Without a word, he gestured to Riley to take the left doorway while he took the right. From here on out, they would have to proceed in silence.

The warehouse was a maze of large, open rooms and smaller offices. Zack could hear the murmur of voices and the drone of a television somewhere. There was a loud crunch—someone eating a potato chip, by the sound of it.

As Zack moved, his mind worked feverishly to cross-reference the blueprints with what lay before them. His heart hammered against his chest, not with fear, but with the relentless drive of the chase. Fisher had been here; the intel was solid.

But now, the prey had vanished.

Where are you, Fisher? Zack thought, frustration simmering beneath his calm exterior. He made his way between the aisles, alert to every creak of the floorboards, every whisper of movement in the air. This was a hunter's game, and he was no stranger to the hunt.

Still, the situation was unnerving.

Suddenly, Zack found himself staring at a set of steps leading down into darkness. He had lost sight of Riley moments ago, their paths diverging in a labyrinth of hallways.

An icy blade of worry sliced through his usual composure. She was more than his partner; she was the one person who could read him without a word spoken, a silent anchor in the chaos of their line of work. Without her, he felt the sharp edge of vulnerability.

She can take care of herself, he reminded himself. *She's one of the most capable people you've ever met.*

With that reminder for comfort, Zack began descending the stairs.

The basement sprawled before him, a vast underground expanse littered with crates and machinery—ghosts of a more productive era. In the far corner, the soft hum of a generator competed with the faint sound of clinking glass.

He moved with deliberate care, each step calculated to avoid detection. The shadows draped around him like a cloak, masking his presence as he closed in on a man standing in the pale glow of a refrigerator's light, a light that illuminated his bare arms.

And the distinct burn scar on the right arm.

Zack edged closer, blending with the darkness that swathed the basement. Fisher, clad in a disheveled shirt that hung loose over worn jeans, was reaching into the fridge for a beer.

Sensing this was his best opportunity, Zack lunged forward, his hand shooting out to clamp down on Fisher's wrist, twisting it behind his back with a practiced maneuver. As he did so, Fisher's hand bumped the beer bottle, causing it to teeter for a suspenseful moment before settling back in place.

Zack sighed inwardly with relief.

"Quiet now, Fisher," he murmured, his voice a low growl. "You and I are going to have a little chat."

"Who the hell—" Fisher started, but Zack pressed the cold muzzle of his gun against the man's temple, silencing him.

Zack changed his tone, speaking into his earpiece. "I've got him, Riley." He paused, waiting, but no answer came. "Riley?"

Something isn't right, he thought, a knot forming in his stomach. Still, he had a job to do. Fear was a distraction, one he couldn't afford—not if he hoped to walk out of this place alive, with or without Fisher.

"Here's how it's gonna go," he told Fisher. "You make any loud noises, and I put a bullet in you. Nod if you understand."

Fisher nodded.

"Good. Now tell me: Why were you at Montrose last night?"

Fisher's eyes darted around the room, searching for an escape that didn't exist. "I wasn't there, man. They fired me two years ago."

"Cut the crap, Fisher." Zack's hand tightened, the gun digging in just a fraction more. "I have you on camera entering the building. How'd you get in, anyway?"

Fisher swallowed, his Adam's apple bobbing nervously. "I...I stole my buddy's badge, okay?"

"Some buddy you are. Why'd you do it?"

"It's not what you think—it had nothing to do with the meltdown, I swear. I was just trying to get my stuff," Fisher stammered, his voice desperate.

"Your stuff?" Zack echoed, a hint of incredulity creeping into his tone. "You risked breaking into a highly monitored building for your 'stuff'? Explain."

Fisher's face twisted in a grimace, his gaze flicking between Zack's cold stare and the gun close to his temple. "There was some…equipment of mine I needed. Things they owed me, especially considering how abruptly they sent me packing."

"Would this 'equipment' include things that could shut down a power plant, by any chance?" Zack pressed, his mind whirring, trying to connect the dots.

"No!" Fisher shook his head vehemently, the movement restricted by Zack's hold. "Just some instruments for measuring radiation, okay?" He sighed, resigning himself to the confession. "Things I could sell to help make ends meet."

"Ah. So you were robbing the place."

Fisher snorted. "Call it what you like. The real robbery took place when they stole my job from me."

Zack thought of a few choice words, but he held them back.

"Besides," Fisher continued, "I was out of there an hour before the meltdown—I can prove it, too." He dug into his pocket, pulling out a crumpled receipt. "I stopped for gas on my way back. See the time signature?"

Zack took the receipt, warily studying it while keeping the gun trained on Fisher. The time signature lined up. It was possible someone else had gotten the receipt...but what were the chances Fisher would've been so prepared to provide an alibi?

Doubt began to gnaw at Zack. Fisher was a small-time crook, not a mastermind. Could he really orchestrate such an attack?

"Why should I believe you?" he asked.

"Because, man," Fisher said, his voice quivering, "I've got a kid. She's just five. I wouldn't do anything that could hurt her or the world she's gonna grow up in."

Zack's grip loosened slightly on Fisher's arm. He hadn't known about the child. Suddenly, his neat and clear-cut world of good and bad began to blur at the edges.

He glanced at the receipt again. The time-stamp was an hour before the meltdown happened, as Fisher had claimed. But that didn’t clear him completely; he could have planted the device and set it off remotely.

Before he could ask another question, however, there was a creak at the top of the stairs.

The voice that cut through the stillness was gruff, laced with the casual menace unique to those accustomed to violence. "Hey, Fisher! You down there?"

Zack grabbed Fisher and guided him behind an old, tattered couch, hiding them from view. Dust motes danced in the shafts of light piercing through the cracked windows, as if mocking their predicament with each carefree swirl.

"Not a sound," Zack whispered fiercely, one hand clamped over Fisher's mouth, the other pressing the cold metal of his gun against the man's ribcage.

Footsteps descended the wooden stairs, each creak a thunderous declaration of their impending discovery.

Zack's mind raced even as he forced his body into statue-like stillness. Every scenario spun out before him—the man finding them, a gunfire ensuing, Riley injured...or worse.

"Come on, man," the voice continued. "I thought you were grabbing a beer." The voice was closer now, almost conversational. He pressed the gun harder into Fisher's side, a silent order for absolute silence.

The seconds stretched on, each heartbeat a drumbeat of tension. Zack's trained eyes stayed locked on the edge of the sofa, watching for any sign of movement. His entire being was coiled like a spring, ready to unleash whatever force necessary to neutralize the threat.

And then, without warning, the man appeared—his shadow falling over them first, a harbinger of doom. A shotgun barrel peeked over the couch, the twin circles of its barrels glaring ominously into Zack's steely gaze.

"Gotcha—" The man's triumphant sneer was cut short as a blur of motion swept from the periphery. The butt of Riley's pistol flew through the air, striking the man in the side of the head. The shotgun clattered to the ground as his body slumped, unconscious before he could register the blow.

"Nice timing," Zack said, the tension bleeding away just enough to allow a twitch of a smile. Riley returned it with a nod, her eyes scanning the room for any more surprises.

"Let's move," she said. Zack nodded, pulling Fisher to his feet with a grip that brooked no argument.

"Stay close," Zack murmured to Riley as he led Fisher up the stairs, then through the labyrinth of corridors above. Each turn was a calculated risk, each doorway an opportunity for ambush. But Zack's senses were fine-tuned instruments; years of training had sharpened them to a razor's edge. His eyes flickered to every corner, every potential hiding spot where danger might lurk.

Zack couldn't shake off the gnawing frustration eating at him. This whole operation was supposed to be a breakthrough. Instead, it was unraveling before his eyes, the threads of certainty fraying into nothingness. They would turn Fisher over to the authorities, but it was a hollow victory, considering what they had set out to accomplish.

They slipped outside, escaping the Black Serpents' notice without any further problems. But as they led Fisher through the woods toward the road where their vehicle waited, Zack found himself wondering: If Fisher had gotten into the power plant by 'borrowing' a friend's badge, how many others might have tried the same thing?

And how many saboteurs might have been there last night to orchestrate the meltdown?

CHAPTER FIVE

Under the heavy shadow of a leaden sky, Zack Force stood at the edge of calamity. The Montrose Nuclear Power Plant loomed like a fallen colossus, its crippled silhouette an omen of unseen terrors that whispered through the air. Walter Hammond, with his grave countenance and weary eyes, was painting a grim picture of the invisible enemy they faced.

"Radiation levels are off the charts," Hammond declared, gesturing to the desolate landscape before them. "The contamination zone extends for miles, a silent killer as lethal as any bomb. Breach that perimeter, and you're signing your own death warrant."

Zack's gaze didn't waver from the smoking ruins. He could almost hear the ghostly echoes of sirens, could envision the chaos that reigned when the plant succumbed to its engineered fate. He felt the unsettling caress of radiation against the protective shell of his resolve.

"Hammond, I understand the risks," Zack said, his voice carrying the weight of his conviction. "But there's a bigger picture here. Someone wanted this to happen. We need to know why—and how they did it."

Riley, standing by his side, fixed him with her steely gaze, the tightness of her mouth hinting at her disapproval. "Zack, it's a suicide mission. Think about what you're walking into. This is not just another case; we're talking about radioactive fallout."

Despite the warning lacing her words, Zack's mind was already infiltrating the dead zone, combing through the wreckage for clues.

"Riley, I have to do this. There could be evidence in there, something everyone else has missed." Zack's tone brokered no argument. It was the voice of a man who'd walked through fire and emerged with only the burns to show for it.

She exhaled, a long, resigned breath that seemed to acknowledge the futility of arguing with him.

"Fine," she conceded, the syllable sharp as a knife's edge. "But if you think for one second that I'm going to let you go in alone, you're crazier than I thought. And Zack? If it gets too dangerous, I'm dragging you out of there, even if I have to knock you unconscious and carry you myself."

"Thanks, Riley," Zack said, allowing himself a brief smile that barely touched his eyes. "Let's hope it doesn't come to that."

"If you really insist on throwing your lives away," Hammond said wearily, "let me at least give you something to wear." He gestured to them, and they followed him into the depths of a nearby mobile command unit. At the back of the unit was a small room filled with Geiger counters, suits, and other radiation-related tools.

"Suit up," Hammond instructed. "Your Geiger counters will be your lifeline. Keep an eye on them."

Zack nodded, stepping into the room lined with bulky hazmat gear hanging like dormant sentinels. The suits, a garish yellow, were a stark contrast to the sterile white of the walls. He hoisted one from its hook, feeling the weight settle in his hands—a tangible reminder of the peril they were about to wade into. As he stepped into the suit, the material crinkled with a sound akin to distant thunder, and the world was muffled into a dull echo chamber.

"Check your seals twice," Riley said, her words slightly distorted through the mask. Her eyes, the only visible part of her face, met his with a mix of resolve and concern.

"Always do," Zack replied, running his gloved fingers over the seams, ensuring no entry point for the invisible killer they were about to confront. He snapped the visor into place with a click that resonated like the chambering of a bullet.

"Remember," Hammond interjected, handing them the Geiger counters, "if those numbers climb too high, you get out. No heroics."

"Understood," Zack said. He glanced at Riley, who gave him a subtle nod, and then they headed out.

The ghostly remains of the Montrose Nuclear Power Plant loomed ahead, a skeletal silhouette against the gray sky. Smoke curled lazily from fissures in the ruins, a serpent's dance that hypnotized with its silent warning.

"Look at this place..." Riley's voice crackled over the radio, a thin thread of awe woven with dread.

"Keep your focus on the readings," Zack reminded her, although his own gaze was riveted to the apocalyptic scene. The plant, once a beacon of energy and progress, now stood as a testament to destruction.

In his mind's eye, the facility was whole again, bustling with workers moving with purpose, unaware that their world was about to shatter. Now, it was as if the earth had opened its maw and devoured all life, leaving behind only this scarred ruin.

The Geiger counter clipped to his belt ticked steadily, a morbid metronome marking time in a place where time itself seemed to hold its breath.

"Zack, what are we actually searching for?" Riley asked.

Zack paused and turned to face her, his eyes bearing the weight of a thousand unspoken thoughts. "I wish I knew exactly," he admitted, the breath fogging up his visor momentarily. "I'm hoping we'll know it when we see it."

Riley nodded, her posture rigid with determination beneath the bulky gear.

As they moved forward, Zack's mind analyzed each detail of the wreckage. His father had taught him that every piece of a puzzle mattered, that it was the small, overlooked fragments that often held the key to unraveling the grand scheme. It wasn't just about protecting the here and now; it was about peeling back the layers of deceit to reveal the truth—to prevent future attempts on the nation's safety.

"Radiation levels are creeping up," Riley warned, breaking into his thoughts. The Geiger counter's rhythm was growing more erratic.

"We're okay for now," he replied, his tone steely. "But keep tracking the readings." He couldn't shake the feeling that they were close, that the answers were hidden somewhere within these charred remains. The thought was both a beacon and a torment, driving him deeper into the contamination zone.

"Maybe this was a mistake," Riley muttered, her concern evident even through the distortion of the hazmat suit's intercom. "We're not finding anything, Zack. Just increasing risk."

He understood her worry. Time was a luxury they didn't have in this irradiated graveyard. But his instincts told him there was something here, something vital that they were missing.

"Let's press on a little longer," he insisted. There was a stubborn streak in him, one that refused to yield in the face of adversity. It was that same tenacity that had seen him through the darkest of times, and it surged within him now, pushing him onward.

They moved through the ruins, the silence punctuated only by the occasional groan of settling debris and the relentless ticking of their Geiger counters. With each passing moment, the atmosphere grew heavier, the weight of potential failure pressing down on Zack.

"Zack, we should head back," Riley said, her voice muffled behind her mask. "We're not finding anything."

"We can't give up now. It's too important."

"More important than our lives? Zack, you know as well as I do the dangers of radiation poisoning. We're pushing our limits, especially given the fact that this is our second time here today."

Zack ground his teeth. He wanted to ignore her or tell her she was wrong, but he knew she was right. This was getting far too dangerous.

Still...could he really go back empty-handed?

That was when he saw it: a hint of leather poking out from beneath a pile of twisted metal and broken concrete. A boot. His heart clenched as a flash of memory, bright and searing as the radioactive material around them, pierced his mind. Once, during his time in Afghanistan, his unit had been ambushed, and a friend of his – Jacob Lockett – had been buried beneath a pile of rubble after an RPG struck the upper half of the building he was standing beside. As the firefight intensified, Zack had tried to locate Jake, but he'd been unable to do so before he was forced to withdraw, along with the rest of his unit.

That was a failure he did not intend to repeat ever again.

"Riley, there's someone here," Zack said as he approached the rubble, his Geiger counter clicking frantically in his hand.

Riley's protest was immediate. "Zack, no! The readings are spiking—it's too dangerous!"

Ignoring her warning, Zack fell to his knees and began tearing at the debris, the protective gloves hindering his dexterity. Each stone removed brought him closer to redemption or madness—he wasn't sure which. Dust filled the air, coating his visor, but he didn't stop, couldn't stop.

"Help me get him out," Zack gasped between breaths, the past blurring with the present, the soldier's boot merging with that of the body trapped under the ruins of the plant. It was getting more and more difficult to breathe—not just because he was over-exerting himself, either. He felt like he was pulling air through a straw.

"Zack, think about what you're doing! We can't help anyone if we're dead!" Riley's voice was a thread of sanity in the chaos, but the pull of duty was stronger. This time, he wouldn't leave a man behind.

"Can't do that," Zack said, his muscles protesting as he heaved a large piece of concrete aside. "This is on me, Riley. Just keep an eye on those counters for me."

Sweat dripped down his forehead, stinging his eyes underneath the mask as he worked. With each movement, he felt the echo of that long-ago day, heard the whispered regrets that had haunted his nights. He would not – could not – let history repeat itself. For his country, for himself, he had to see this through.

Zack's hands were trembling, but it wasn't only from the exertion. The Geiger counter clipped to his suit was chirping distressingly, the ominous *tick-tick-tick* accelerating like the heartbeat of a frightened animal. He could feel the invisible threat all around him, the toxic legacy of human error underlined by malice. But there was a body under this wreckage, someone who had been a man with dreams and fears, and now he was nothing more than a silent witness to catastrophe.

"Radiation levels are still climbing, Zack," Riley said, alarmed. "We're getting into the red zone."

"Almost there," he replied, his voice hoarse as he knelt beside the partially uncovered form. The detritus that entombed the victim – a twisted mass of concrete, plastic, and unidentifiable debris – had become less daunting after relentless minutes of digging. With one final heave, Zack cleared the last large obstruction, revealing the body fully. It was a heavyset man dressed in what once must have been the uniform of a plant worker, now charred and ragged.

Zack was already feeling lightheaded as he slid his arms under the corpse. He paused, taking a moment to catch his breath.

"Zack, look at this," Riley called out. Her flashlight beam settled on a panel on the wall. The panel door stood open, and inside, amidst the tangle of wires, hung the broken remains of a small handheld device—little more than a piece of cracked plastic attached to a few circuit boards.

"Don't think this belongs here," Riley murmured, pulling the device free and turning it over in her gloved hands. "Could be something used by the saboteurs."

"Grab it and let's move," Zack ordered.

Zack's muscles burned with a fiery intensity as he hoisted the heavy body over his shoulder. His vision went black for a moment, then cleared. As he trudged forward, his boots sinking slightly into the ash-covered ground, he told himself he was fine. It was just the fear of radiation that was getting to him. He could power through it, as he always did.

"Let me help you with him," Riley said. "Zack, you don't have to—"

"I've got it," he said.

As they moved away from the contamination zone, the smoking ruins began to fade into the backdrop, replaced by the increasingly familiar landscape of emergency vehicles and frenzied activity.

Suddenly, Zack's vision started to blur at the edges again, the world tilting ever so slightly with each labored breath. Why was it so difficult to breathe? Was it just his imagination, or was something wrong with his suit?

"Zack, your vitals are spiking," Riley said, her voice now sharp with anxiety. "You need to slow down before—"

The ground seemed to lurch beneath him, and Zack's heart hammered against his ribcage. A dizzy spell washed over him, a rogue wave threatening to drag him under. He stumbled, the dead man's weight becoming an anchor, and his vision swam with images of past battles, of faces lost and lives sacrificed. He fought against it, clenching his teeth to stave off the nausea that clawed at his insides.

"Damn it, Zack!" Riley cried.

The world spun, colors bleeding together into a maelstrom of disorientation. With a herculean effort, he planted one foot in front of the other, determined not to succumb.

But the strength that had always been his fortress now crumbled like the walls of a breached citadel. Zack's knees buckled, and he collapsed to the ground, the body rolling off his shoulder as darkness rushed in to claim him.

CHAPTER SIX

The sterile scent of antiseptic filled the air, mingling with the faint hum of medical machinery as Zack lay in a standard-issue hospital bed, feeling steadier than before but still not quite himself. He felt hollowed out, weak.

A flickering screen mounted to the wall opposite his bed showed images of emergency responders clad in hazmat suits, and evacuees with nothing but the clothes on their backs escaping nearby towns. The anchor's voice was a distant drone, reporting the rising numbers—casualties, missing persons, those touched by the invisible hand of radiation poisoning.

Zack's jaw clenched. He hated lying here, feeling helpless.

"Well, don't you look as cheerful as a bull with a thorn in its side."

Riley Carter stood in the doorway, her silhouette framed by the fluorescent lights of the hallway. A rare smile played across her lips, a stark contrast to the gravity of her usual demeanor.

"What happened?" he asked.

"Suit malfunction."

"That explains why I couldn't breathe. How'd it malfunction?"

"Apparently, one of the fittings was loose. The suit hadn't been worn in a while."

Zack grunted. That tiny oversight had nearly cost him his life. Still, there was no point in getting hung up on it.

He glanced down at Riley's hands. She was holding an object covered in wrapping paper, a ribbon jauntily tied atop.

"Thought you could use a pick-me-up," she said, extending the mystery package toward him.

He took it, fingers brushing against hers, and the subtle warmth of her skin was grounding. With deliberate care, he peeled away the paper, revealing a chessboard crafted from polished oak, its white squares intricately lined with silver. The accompanying pieces, wrapped in a separate layer of paper, were carved from black and white stone. It was a magnificent set, one that harkened back to the bygone era of kings and knights.

"The game has survived centuries of war, plagues, and even world-altering catastrophes," Riley said. "I thought...maybe it would bring a little perspective."

Zack looked up at her, his gaze meeting hers in a quiet understanding. The corners of his mouth turned upwards in a faint smile, and he reached for a carved knight. He could feel the cool marble under his fingertips, the intricate details etched into the tiny horse's mane and the raised leg as if it was about to leap off its perch.

"I suppose it's a good reminder that life goes on," he murmured, rotating the knight in his fingers. His smile was genuine but subtle, the kind only those who knew him well could read.

"There's a second meaning, too," she said, pressing her lips together in a thin, serious line. "You have to play the long game, Zack—and that means being careful. I know you don't want to hear it, but it's true."

He took a deep breath and let it out slowly. "Duly noted. But I can't just lie here, waiting for someone else to do the work I should be doing. I should be in the field, not lying here helplessly."

"Stubborn as ever," she said with a sigh, but there was no real bite to her words. "Take it from someone who knows a thing or two about patience." Her NYPD days, he knew she meant. Those hard-earned lessons she brought with her into every investigation.

The faint beep of the heart monitor was a metronomic underscore to Zack's thoughts as his mind began to wander. His eyes, though heavy-lidded from pain medication, were alert and searching as Riley settled into the chair beside him, her presence an anchor in the sea of clinical white.

"The body I found at Montrose..." Zack began uncertainly. "Have we ID'd him?"

She nodded, her features softening with compassion. "We did. His name was Dr. Eliot Harper, a lead engineer for the power plant. Came from a small town in Ohio; brilliant mind, loved by his community."

The news pierced through Zack's foggy consciousness, sharpening his focus. A man who had dedicated his life to the safe harnessing of power, now a casualty of its catastrophic release.

"His family?" Zack asked.

"Grateful. Devastated, but grateful," Riley said gently, her hand reaching out to rest atop his. "Because of you, they're not left wondering. They have closure, Zack."

Zack turned his gaze to the window, where the D.C. skyline was etched against the afternoon light. Dr. Harper would be returned home, his memory honored, his absence forever felt. It was a cold comfort, but it was something—a testament to the fact that even in the darkest ruins, dignity could still be salvaged.

"What about the device you found?" Zack asked, his voice a notch firmer as he shifted back to the practicalities.

"Sent it to Neil Masterson," Riley said. "If anyone can make sense of it, it's him. Still waiting to hear back."

Zack nodded. Inwardly, though, he hated the idea of waiting a moment longer. Every second that ticked by was another second the saboteurs remained shrouded in mystery. Another second they could be planning their next move. He clenched his jaw, the desire to leap into action coursing through his veins, tempered only by the reality of his battered body.

Just then, Riley's phone rang. Zack watched as her face morphed into professional mode, her body language shifting subtly. She answered with a curt 'Carter' and listened intently, her gaze never leaving Zack. As she spoke in terse affirmatives, Zack's own focus

"Director Liz wants to see us," Riley said once the call had ended, pocketing the phone.

"Good," Zack replied, pushing back the thin blanket and swinging his legs over the side of the bed, ignoring the protest from his battered body. "Let's go."

"Zack, you're in no shape to—" Riley began, but he cut her off with a look.

"Riley, I can't just sit here while—" he grunted, standing up with effort, "—while everything falls apart out there."

"Fine," she said, knowing better than to argue when he had that fire in his eyes. "But if you pass out on me, I'm dragging your ass back here myself."

He gave her a half-smile, one that didn't quite reach his eyes. "Deal."

* * *

The conference room was austere, its long table surrounded by faces etched with concern and authority. Zack took measured steps beside Riley, each footfall a defiance against the ache in his muscles. The air was silent, expectant.

"I thought this was supposed to be meeting with the director," Zack murmured to Riley.

She gave him a subtle shrug, as if to say she'd thought the same.

"Agent Force, glad you could join us," a man with a hawkish nose and deep-set eyes said from the head of the table. It was General Hawthorne, a man known for his hardliner views on security. Zack had heard his name in passing but never met him personally.

His tone was a mix of thinly veiled contempt and genuine appreciation, as though Zack's presence was both a matter of irritation and necessity. "We've been discussing the situation at hand," he continued, gesturing to Riley. "Agent Carter has already filled us in on some of the details."

Sitting down, Zack let his gaze sweep across the room, noting the grim faces around him, expressions etched with exhaustion and concern."What I don't understand," Hawthorne continued crisply, "is why you thought it was a good idea to endanger your lives – not once, but twice – in an active radiation zone."

Zack met the General's icy stare, his voice steady. "Because, sir," he began, "that's our job. To put ourselves on the line in order to protect and serve. Agent Carter and I did what was necessary."

"Is that so?" the general murmured, not backing down. "You ever heard of drones, hmm?"

"Sir," Riley interrupted, "with all due respect, we assessed the situation and used our best judgment. If we'd had drones on standby, we might very well have used them. But we didn't."

The general did not reply.

Zack's jaw clenched as he faced the room, each official a blur of disdain framed by the stark, sterile walls of the conference room—all but Liz, who gazed back at him with...what? Sympathy?

"Look," Zack began, his voice like gravel, grinding against the silence, "that device we recovered could be the key to understanding who's behind this attack." The officials appeared unmoved, their expressions a barricade against his urgency.

"Perhaps," he continued, his voice growing louder, "you may think we are reckless, but let's remember the fact that we are not dealing with common criminals here. They took down a nuclear power plant, for goodness' sake. And they are still out there. I am willing to take whatever risks necessary to stop them. Wouldn't you do the same if you were in my shoes?"

There was a pause, and then the general spoke again, his voice measured and devoid of any emotion. "We are here to evaluate the situation, Agent Force, not question your bravado or courage."

Zack clenched his fists under the table but said nothing.

Another official, Randy Stone, an older man with a bushy gray mustache, cleared his throat and leaned forward. "As interesting as that device may be, Agent Force, there's no guarantee it has anything whatsoever to do with the attack. It could be a perfectly innocent tool used by someone on staff—we just don't know."

"Even so," Zack countered, voice steady in the face of the man's skepticism. "It's a lead. The only one we have."

"We aren't disputing that," Stone replied, his tone softer than Hawthorne's had been. "But taking unnecessary risk—"

"Is part of our jobs," Zack snapped. The room seemed to constrict around him, the fluorescent lights above casting a harsh glare over the faces of those who dared to belittle his findings. He felt discarded, his efforts tossed aside like the rubble he'd sifted through only hours earlier.

He felt Director Liz Murdock's gaze on him, probing, searching.

General Hawthorne smiled thinly. "I'm beginning to think you should still be in that hospital bed, Agent Force. Maybe we should resume this conversation when you're more...composed."

"And maybe we should resume this conversation when you've stepped foot in a radiation zone, general," Zack shot back.

The silence that followed was absolute, hanging heavy in the austere room. Hawthorne's smile vanished, replaced with an icy glare Zack met without a flinch. Tension crackled through the room like an electrical current.

"That's enough," Liz said sharply. "Agent Force, I'll speak with you outside."

Stifling the fury building within him, Zack took a breath, his gaze lingering on Director Murdock before he turned sharply on his heel and strode out. The door swung closed with a resounding thud behind him, cutting off the murmurs that erupted in his wake.

In the corridor outside, Zack allowed the mask of his anger to slip. He leaned against the cold, impersonal steel paneling of the wall, pressing his forehead against it as he fought for composure. The silence out here was a stark contrast to the barrage of criticism that had just been leveled at him inside, and it was sobering.

The door swung open behind him with a creak, Liz stepping through. Her brows were furrowed in worry, her usually sharp eyes softer now with concern as she looked at his visibly shaken form. She offered no words of empty comfort, no assurances or soothing platitudes. She knew him too well for that.

"You can't lose your cool like that," she said after a heavy pause, her voice a gentle reprimand. "General Hawthorne is looking for any reason to discredit you, Zack. I think he sees a younger version of himself in you, and it threatens him."

Zack rubbed his eyes with the heels of his palms. "We risked our lives out there, Liz. For what? For them to dismiss it like it was nothing?"

Liz leaned against the wall beside him, her gaze steady on the opposite side of the corridor. "It's not nothing. But it's their job to think in terms of resources and feasibility."

"But they don't understand—"

"And they won't, not from you yelling at them." She sighed. "Listen, Zack, you're putting yourself through a lot. You need to be careful."

Zack said nothing.

"That device," Liz said after a few moments. "You really think it's important, don't you?"

"It could be the key to this investigation," Zack said, the frustration ebbing as he looked into her eyes, finding an understanding that had been absent in the conference room.

"Then we'll pursue this, but carefully," Liz continued, her words measured, steeped in years of navigating treacherous waters. "We can't afford any missteps. Your father...he taught you well. He'd be proud of how you're handling this."

Zack felt something unclench within him at her words. Here was validation—a recognition of his efforts that mattered more than the scorn of a dozen bureaucrats. Liz Murdock wasn't just his superior; she was a remnant of his father's legacy, a beacon in the tumultuous world he navigated. Her confidence in him steeled his resolve.

"Thank you, Director," he said, the title spoken with genuine respect. "I won't let this go. Not while there's a chance to stop them."

"Good," Liz nodded once, decisively. "But you have to be discreet about this. I know you're not one for playing politics, but we have to navigate this minefield carefully."

He met her gaze, his jaw set. Her eyes held that same sharp intelligence that always seemed to pierce through the fog of bureaucracy.

"Remember," she continued, "sometimes the quietest moves are the most effective. Don't let your emotions control you. Use them as fuel, but do not let them steer the ship."

The door to the conference room swung open just then, and Riley strode out.

"Got a message from Neil," she said, her tone urgent. A lock of her dark hair fell across her face as she looked up from her phone. "He's been working on the device non-stop. Says it's definitely linked to the saboteurs—not something that would have any legitimate use in a nuclear power plant."

Zack frowned, absorbing this news. "Did he learn anything else?"

"Yes." She paused, hesitating. "According to Neil, the tech involved is very sophisticated—cutting edge, you might say. It wasn't built by some disgruntled engineer in his basement." She paused, as if bracing herself for what she was about to say next.

"Which makes me wonder if it's only the prelude to something worse."

CHAPTER SEVEN

"It's chaos, Mr. Force," Felicity Malek, the Head of Personnel at Montrose, said as she clutched a list of employees like a lifeline, her voice a taut wire of stress. "Several of our staff haven't reported since the incident. It's...it's making it near impossible to account for everyone."

Zack leaned forward, resting his elbows on the makeshift desk of the mobile workstation, his eyes never leaving Felicity's. "We need to know who was here, Felicity. It's imperative to find out if this was an inside job."

She hesitated. "Do you have reason to believe it was an inside job?"

"Galen Fisher," he said, the name tasting bitter.

"Who?"

"Someone you fired two years ago. He admitted to using someone else's badge to access the plant after he was terminated."

"Last night?"

Zack nodded. "But we've already cleared him of any wrongdoing in this. I'd like you to tell me about your security measures. Is it possible others could've exploited the same loophole?"

Felicity's fingers drummed on the desk, a staccato echo of uncertainty. "Our security is stringent. Badges, biometrics, random checks. But..." She sighed, looking away. "No system is foolproof. There's always human error, misplaced trust. If someone wanted to get in badly enough, they might find a way."

Zack's jaw clenched as he absorbed this information. He wasn't entirely surprised, but it was frustrating nonetheless. The saboteurs could've fled the country by now, and if they were clever enough to use false identities, then nobody would know they weren't still buried in the rubble of the power plant.

"Zack!" Riley's voice sliced through his thoughts, urgent and edged with something he couldn't quite place. "You need to see this."

He turned toward her, noting the tight set of her jaw, the way her eyes were locked onto the screen before her. She swiveled the monitor in his direction, revealing a news alert that splashed the words 'BREAKING NEWS' in blood-red letters against a backdrop of night.

"Leading nuclear physicist Angela Horowitz has been reported missing from her San Francisco home," the crisply dressed reporter was saying, her tone suggesting a mix of concern and excitement at the story unfolding before her. "According to her neighbors, Horowitz hasn't been seen since late last night, and police have found signs of a struggle in her apartment."

Zack's mind went into overdrive, connecting dots in rapid succession. Angela Horowitz, nuclear physicist, missing from San Francisco. She was one of the highest-profile scientists in the field, known for her work on experimental reactors that promised cleaner, safer energy. If she was connected to the incident at Montrose…

He looked back at Felicity. "Did Horowitz ever visit Montrose?"

Felicity’s eyes widened. "Yes...yes, she did. She consulted on our reactor design."

An image of Angela Horowitz filled the screen—a woman with sharp features and intelligent eyes that seemed to stare back at him with an accusation he had yet to understand.

"The timing is too coincidental to ignore," Riley said.

"We need to find out what she was working on," Zack said.

"Could be the same group behind both incidents," Riley said, her fingers already dancing across the keyboard as she opened new tabs, searching for any digital footprint Dr. Horowitz may have left behind.

"Dig up everything you can." Zack's gaze remained fixed on the screen, watching as the report transitioned to amateur footage from outside Horowitz's residence—police tape fluttering like spectral ribbons in the night breeze. "We need to know who would benefit from taking her."

"Will do." Riley didn't miss a beat. "But Zack, if they're targeting leading figures in nuclear science…"

"Then we're not just dealing with an isolated event," Zack finished for her, the gravity of the situation settling into his bones. "There's no telling how many other plants they might target."

"Exactly." Riley met his gaze, her expression grim. "And whoever orchestrated this has a larger endgame in mind."

Aware that Felicity was still in the room, Zack gave her a curt nod. "Thanks for your help. You may go now."

Felicity nodded back, looking a bit flustered as she rose. She paused, as if contemplating saying something more, and then hurried.

The glow from Zack’s laptop cast a pale light on his face as he sifted through Ms. Horowitz's published papers, her symposium keynotes, her speaking events. It was the gaps, however, the redacted lines in her employment history, that intrigued him most.

"Working on something big, weren't you, Ms. Horowitz?" Zack muttered to himself.

Riley stood over his shoulder, the reflection of scrolling text flickering in her eyes. "Any luck?"

"More than luck," he replied, zooming in on a document so heavily blacked out it was more redaction than revelation. "She was deep into something classified. It's got the stink of state secrets all over it."

"Sounds like we're going to San Francisco, then." Riley's tone was flat, her fingers drumming against her arm.

"One of us is, anyway."

Riley gave him a quizzical look. "What are you talking about?"

"I want you to stay here," he said. "This is still ground zero, and I need someone I can trust right here, where the attack happened."

"They're not going to attack here again."

"No, probably not. But that doesn't mean there isn't evidence to gather. I want you to continue looking into the employees, see if you can figure out who did this."

"Zack, I don’t like this," she said, catching his gaze. "Splitting up now? It feels wrong."

"Can't be helped," Zack said, standing up and stretching his muscular frame. "I need you here, Riley. And I need to be on the ground in San Francisco."

She looked like she was about to argue, her features hardening, but then she sighed and rolled her shoulders. "Alright. For now. But you're keeping me updated every step of the way."

"You got it," Zack said, already moving toward the door. The urgency in his gut wouldn't let him sit still any longer.

"And watch your back!" she called. "Pretend like I'm there to watch it for you, okay?"

He smiled. "I'm sure I'll have your nagging voice in my head every step of the way."

* * *

Zack strode across the tarmac, his senses alert despite the late hour. The airstrip was quiet, save for the gentle hum of the private plane's engines warming up. He had expected solitude, a moment to gather his thoughts before the flight, but instead he found an idling SUV, its headlights cutting through the nighttime mist.

As he approached, the passenger door swung open, and Liz stepped out, her presence commanding even in the dim light. Beside her emerged a young woman, about Zack's age, with sharp features and an analytical gaze that immediately began dissecting him.

"Zack Force," Liz said by way of greeting, "meet Maya Walsh. FBI."

"Profiler," Maya added, extending her hand in a firm handshake.

"Didn't realize we were bringing in the Feds," Zack said, masking his surprise. He sized her up, noting the confidence in her stance, the keen edge to her eyes.

"Actually," Maya said, "it's the other way around."

Zack raised a quizzical eyebrow and glanced at Liz.

"Maya's been working on the Horowitz case from their end," Liz explained. "And now, you two will work it together."

"Is that right?" There was an edge to Zack's voice, a hint of resistance to the imposition. "I prefer working alone."

"This isn't about what you prefer," Liz said. "It's about finding Horowitz and stopping whoever's behind this."

Maya stepped forward. "I understand your reservations," she said. "But I've been profiling individuals connected to Horowitz since she went missing. I know their methods, their motivations. I'm not here to step on your toes; I'm here to help you find her faster."

Zack looked at Maya, really looked at her for the first time. Her eyes were sharp, her stance confident yet non-threatening. She wasn't just some suit sent to babysit him; she was a weapon in her own right.

Zack wanted to argue, to insist on his lone wolf methods, but he saw the determination in Liz's eyes and knew there was no room for debate. He glanced at Maya again, her intense gaze now softened with something akin to sympathy, as if she too had been thrust into this unwanted partnership.

"All right," Zack finally agreed, letting out a resigned sigh. "Welcome aboard, Ms. Walsh."

Liz gestured toward the plane. "Your transport is ready. We've arranged everything."

Zack nodded. "Let's not waste any more time, then."

Zack's heartbeat got a little faster as he approached the sleek jet, a charcoal silhouette against the inky sky. The air was tinged with jet fuel and anticipation.

"Nice evening for flying," Maya ventured, her voice slicing the quiet that hung between them. The comment dangled in the air, unacknowledged, as they ascended the stairs into the belly of the plane.

Inside, the cabin was awash with the plush comforts of high-end travel, but no amount of luxury could ease the tension that bristled like static in the small space. Zack chose a seat by the window, his gaze fixed on the dark horizon as the engines rumbled to life. Maya sat opposite, her presence an enigma wrapped in an FBI badge.

"Ever been to San Francisco before?" she asked.

"Business, never pleasure," Zack replied tersely, his eyes never leaving the view outside. The words hung heavy, a bridge neither of them were ready to cross.

As the plane climbed through the dusk, the silence settled around them again, punctuated only by the occasional clink of ice in a glass or the soft rustle of Maya shifting in her seat.

"Look," Maya said after a long stretch of quiet, unfolding a file and laying it out on the table between them, "I know we're both used to running our own shows, but I've got a good profile started on Horowitz. Maybe you can make use of it."

Zack's eyes flicked to the documents, then back to the window. His fingers itched to rifle through the pages, to extract every morsel of information, but he was wary of this sort of partnership. He knew all too well how much interagency politics could interfere with investigations, and the last thing he wanted was for this to become a matter of who got the credit.

Despite his misgivings, however, he found himself unable to resist the urge to study the top sheet. It was detailed, thorough—exactly what he would have expected from the FBI.

"Maya," he said, breaking the silence once more as he met her gaze across the narrow aisle. Her eyes, keen and expectant, held his. "Let's make a deal, shall we?"

"I'm listening."

"You don't get in my way, and I won't get in yours. I don't want this to become a tug-of-war, each of us competing for control of the investigation."

She paused to consider. "I don't want that either, Zack. We're on the same team."

"Sure," Zack responded, noncommittal. "For now we are. And then, once we've found Ms. Horowitz, I'll go my way and you go yours."

"Fair enough," Maya said, giving a single nod.

Zack sighed, turning his attention to the document now in his hands. "Let's just hope your profile helps us find Ms. Horowitz—*before* whoever kidnapped her is done with her."

CHAPTER EIGHT

It was the fluttering police tape that caught Zack's eye as he and Maya approached Angela Horowitz's house in the heart of San Francisco.

That, and the silence. The police had already finished their investigation, and the usual buzz of the city seemed to have respectfully hushed itself. The only sound now was the distant hum of a cable car, its bells cutting mournfully through the fog-shrouded streets.

Zack parked the black sedan along the street and turned off the engine, pausing to study the neighborhood. The Victorian row houses, with their ornate wooden accents and regal shades of pastel, should have looked charming in the gentle post-rain light. But now they appeared like silent tombstones, standing vigil over a tragedy that they had been helpless to prevent.

The agents left the car and approached the house. As they entered the house, the disarray struck Zack—a chair overturned, papers scattered like the aftermath of a storm, clear indications of a struggle.

"Angela fought back, alright," Maya said, taking in the scene.

Zack nodded, his gaze traveling from the shattered vase by the fireplace to the scuffs on the hardwood floor. "Quite desperately, too, I'd say," he said quietly, feeling a surge of respect for the missing physicist. "Whatever happened, Angela didn't make it easy for them."

Zack's eyes swept the room, a silent sentinel as he processed the disarray: the aftermath of panic and violence. The ambiance of Angela Horowitz's home felt thick with unanswered questions, every overturned chair a mute witness to her abduction.

"I've got the entry point," Maya said, her fingers tracing the jagged edges where the frame of the back door had given way. "Brute force—looks like they just smashed their way in and grabbed her. No subtlety needed."

"No fear of the neighbors hearing," Zack murmured. "They probably figured they'd be in and out in a few seconds, but they didn't count on the physicist fighting back the way she did."

Maya nodded. "Let's just hope she hasn't suffered too much for it."

Zack studied the room again, trying to figure out what Angela had been doing when she was attacked. He walked toward the toppled chair that sat by the grand oak desk, a cascade of papers surrounding it. He knelt down, careful not to disturb anything, and picked up a sheet from the top of the pile. It was filled with complex equations and notations that a layman would find incomprehensible, but to Angela Horowitz, it was her life's work.

"In the middle of something," Zack murmured, his gaze now scanning the room for more clues. "Maybe she saw them coming?"

"Or heard them," Maya suggested, now examining the shattered vase near the fireplace. She crouched low, studying something in particular. She reached out carefully with gloved hands and picked up a shard of glass. "Blood."

Zack's eyes met Maya's. "Angela's?"

Maya tilted her head thoughtfully as she examined the shard. "Could be," she said after a moment. "Or could belong to one of them. We'll have to get it to the lab to find out."

Zack nodded and turned his attention back to the oak desk. "Where's her computer?" he murmured.

"FBI already confiscated it. Government secrets and all."

Zack nodded absently and continued looking around. His gaze fell on a bookshelf by the fireplace. A number of the books had fallen on the floor, revealing something peculiar along the shelf: a scuff mark, as if from a moving part.

Zack rose from his spot near the desk and made his way toward the fireplace. With Maya watching from her position by the door, he studied the scuff mark, tracing it with his gloved finger, right to left. He paused, looking thoughtful. "There's a secret compartment in here," he murmured.

Maya raised an eyebrow as she joined him at the bookshelf. "What makes you say that?"

Zack gestured at the empty shelf. "This scuff mark—the panel clearly swings out." He tilted his head and squinted at the titles on the spines of the remaining books. “A classic mystery setup.”

Maya grinned. "You've been watching too many old detective movies."

"Maybe," Zack said with a half-smile as he scanned the titles again. His gaze fell on an old physics book: ‘Wave-Particle Duality’. Angela was a physicist after all, and given her penchant for paradoxes, it felt fitting.

He reached out and pulled at the book. The board behind the book came with it, revealing a small box filled with a number of personal items: some jewelry, a pair of vintage spectacles, a few faded photographs, an odd, metallic object that looked vaguely like a miniature astrolabe…

But what caught Zack's attention more than the rest was the small notebook.

Zack pulled the notebook out and opened it. There were only a few pages inside, each one written in a complex, cryptic shorthand Zack couldn't make any sense of.

"Looks like she was trying to keep something very secret," Maya said.

"Probably notes about whatever classified project she was working on," Zack said.

"Think it's related to what happened at Montrose?"

"That's what I want to find out." He pulled out his phone. "I know someone – Neil Masterson – who's good with this sort of thing. He has software that can—"

Just then, Zack heard a floorboard creak in the hallway. He froze, every muscle tensing, his trained senses heightening. The phone remained poised in mid-air, the call to Neil unsent.

"Did you hear that?" Maya's voice was barely a whisper, but it resonated like a gunshot in the sudden stillness.

"Stay quiet," he mouthed, his eyes locking with hers as he shoved the notebook into his pocket. His hand motioned subtly toward the rear of the house as he grasped the cold metal of the gun at his side. This was familiar territory for him, the adrenaline rush of potential confrontation.

Zack moved toward the sound, each step deliberate, the floorboards beneath him mercifully silent. His heart pounded against his ribcage, a rhythm that matched the ticking clock of urgency in his mind.

The footsteps were careful, almost imperceptible, but to a man like Zack, they screamed an alarm. He was acutely aware of Maya taking cover behind the leather couch, her own weapon drawn. The dance they performed was one of life and death, choreographed by instinct and training.

Zack reached the back door without incident. It was ajar, just slightly.

The hairs on the back of Zack's neck stood on end. Instinct screamed at him to duck, and he did so just as a figure lunged from the darkness, a flash of metal glinting in the dim light. Zack rolled away, narrowly avoiding the blade that whooshed past where his head had been moments before.

Zack grunted as he blocked a punch, feeling the sting of impact against his forearm. He countered with a right hook, putting every ounce of his rural Alabama strength into the blow. The man staggered, but didn't fall. They were locked in combat now, each move a brutal dance of survival.

Then, amid the grunts and thuds of their struggle, Zack heard it—gunshots piercing the stillness of the house. There were others.

"Maya!" he called out, tearing his attention from the assailant for a split second—a mistake. The masked man saw his chance and tackled Zack, sending them both crashing to the ground.

But Zack Force was no stranger to a fight. With a swift motion, he flipped the attacker off him and delivered a punishing kick that sent the man sprawling. He needed to get to Maya.

He sprinted back to the main room, his heartbeat thundering in his ears. As he burst into the space, he saw Maya crouched by the window, firing off controlled shots at a figure crouched behind a stone wall.

Zack reached for his phone to call for backup, but there was no signal. Scrambled.

His gut clenched; they were isolated, cut off from the world.

"Damn it," he cursed under his breath, holstering the useless device. His mind raced, piecing together the implications. "They're jamming us. They came prepared."

Zack's pulse hammered in his ears—a relentless drumbeat that underscored the grim reality of their situation. As Maya reloaded, her movements deft and sure despite the chaos, he tallied the masked figures moving with military precision outside. There were too many. Like dark wraiths, they converged on Angela's house with one purpose—to keep them from leaving.

"Maya," Zack said, his voice low and urgent, "we can't take them all. We need to extract."

"Back to the car?" She swiveled toward him, eyes sharp as flint.

"Exactly." The vehicle was armored, a small fortress compared to their current vulnerable position. "I'll cover you. Move fast."

"Got it." Her nod was terse, the motion of one warrior syncing up with another.

As Maya sprinted for the door, Zack stepped into the breach and began firing. Bullets ricocheted off the walls, sending plaster dust sprinkling over his hair like graying confetti. This was not how he had envisioned today unfolding when they touched down in San Francisco;

this was supposed to be a search, not a siege. But adapting was what he did best.

It was what kept him alive.

He caught sight of Maya reaching the vehicle, her silhouette a beacon of success amidst the gunfire. Now it was his turn. With a deep breath that tasted of grit and resolve, Zack bolted from the cover of the house.

The ground erupted around him, geysers of dirt and concrete marking the passage of bullets seeking flesh. His heart was a wild thing, thrashing against its ribcage, his mind a swirling vortex where only survival mattered.

"Come on, Force," he muttered through gritted teeth, the mantra of his own survival blending with the cacophony of battle.

The vehicle loomed ahead, a bastion amidst the storm. As he threw himself behind the wheel, bullets punched through the windows, showering him in chunks of glass. Maya was already in the passenger seat, gun at the ready, her profile etched with determination.

"Drive!" she shouted, her voice slicing through the thunderous noise.

The engine roared to life under Zack's command, a growling beast eager to flee the madness. They peeled away from the curb, chased by a hail of bullets.

CHAPTER NINE

Zack's hands gripped the steering wheel with white-knuckled intensity, each turn of the vehicle a calculated escape through the tight arteries of San Francisco's streets. The city, usually vibrant and pulsating with life, now felt like an intricate maze designed to ensnare them.

He cast a sidelong glance at Maya, noting her focus as she tapped her phone screen in a futile attempt to call for backup.

"Are you hit?" Zack's voice was steady despite the adrenaline coursing through his veins.

Maya shook her head, her eyes briefly meeting his before returning to her device. "No, I'm good. But this is useless," she grumbled, clicking the phone off and on again, trying to break through whatever was jamming their signal.

"Keep trying. It might work once we put some distance between us and them," Zack said, accelerating as they approached a busy intersection, the honk of horns joining the cacophony of the chase. His mind worked feverishly, analyzing routes and potential safe zones as he tried to recall their drive from the airport.

The streets blurred past, storefronts and pedestrians merging into a busy watercolor that stained the edges of Zack's vision. He swerved around a delivery truck, earning a screech of brakes and angry shouts that dissipated into the air behind them. The pulse in his ears drowned out the noise of the city, and for a moment, it was just him, the car, and the relentless mission that drove him forward.

Just then, Zack glanced into the rearview mirror and spotted a white van barreling after them.

The rearview mirror became a portal to Zack's nightmare as he spied the glint of steel and desperation.

"Looks like they're not giving up just yet," he said.

A figure leaned out of the passenger window of the van and aimed an automatic weapon at them.

"Get down!" Zack shouted, grabbing Maya's shoulder and pushing her forward as the automatic went off. A few bullets punched into the metal frame of the vehicle, and one tore through the edge of Zack's seat, narrowly missing his head.

"Can't you lose them?" Maya cried.

"Working on it!" he answered, veering sharply to avoid a spray of bullets that kissed the tarmac where they'd been seconds ago. The chase was a blur of color and sound, the world reduced to the binary of predator and prey.

As they careened toward Fisherman's Wharf, the scent of saltwater and seafood was overshadowed by the stench of burning rubber and fear. Zack's heart thudded against his ribs like a drumbeat of war, each pulse synchronous with the thrumming engine. They were running out of road and time, but surrender wasn't part of Zack Force's vocabulary.

"Zack, watch out!"

He didn't need the warning. Instinct had already propelled him into a hard left, tires screeching in protest as they narrowly avoided a collision with a tram. Onlookers scattered, their screams lost to the wind, faces blurring into a single tapestry of shock and awe. It was a spectacle ripped from the pages of a Hollywood script, yet every jolt, every near miss, was undeniably real.

"Keep your head down," he barked at Maya, but she was already crouched low. He admired her calm, the way she processed the situation not with panic, but with analytical precision. It was that same unflappable nature that might just see them through this alive.

The air was thick with the salty tang of the bay, and the scent of fresh seafood from the open-air markets mingled with the odors of brine and diesel, creating an olfactory tapestry unique to the waterfront. Zack gripped the steering wheel tighter as they careened around a corner, narrowly avoiding a vendor's cart loaded with apples.

"Left here, there's an alley!" Maya shouted over the din of screeching tires.

Zack yanked the wheel, and the car lurched into the narrow passage. Graffiti-stained walls formed a tight corridor, a stark contrast to the open vistas of the city they'd left behind. The sound of their pursuers was a constant thunder, a storm on their heels that refused to abate.

"Keep going," Maya urged, her gaze fixed on the rearview mirror. "They're still on us."

"Like hell they are," Zack muttered under his breath.

As they emerged back onto the main road, the iconic signs of the Wharf loomed before them, a beacon of normalcy that seemed almost surreal given their circumstances. Tourists ambled, blissfully unaware of the danger approaching, a danger that Zack and Maya carried with them like a maelstrom.

"Watch out!" Maya's warning came just as a black SUV barreled into view, its windows down, revealing the cold gleam of firearms.

Zack swerved, the car fishtailing wildly. Bullets whizzed past them, some finding their mark with thuds against the vehicle's already battered frame. Adrenaline surged through Zack's veins, a burning fire that fueled his reflexes. He was the eye of the storm, calm yet lethal, every move calculated with surgical precision.

"Zack, we can't lead them into the crowd!"

He knew she was right—they couldn't risk civilian casualties. But options were dwindling fast, and the space to maneuver was closing in like a vice. And then, fate twisted the knife—a loud pop, a jolt, and the car began to list dangerously to one side.

"Damn it!" Zack cursed as the blown-out tire rendered the vehicle all but useless. They limped forward a short distance before Zack, realizing they wouldn't be going anywhere in a hurry, spun the wheel to the side and aimed for an alley, slamming on his brakes so that the vehicle would block the alley while he and Maya made their escape on foot.

They burst from the car, hitting the ground running. Zack didn't hear any sounds of pursuit just yet, but he knew better than to think they'd given up.

"Down here!" Maya pointed toward a set of stairs leading to the water's edge.

They descended the stairs two at a time, the metal clanging beneath their footsteps. The pier stretched out before them, a dead end that offered neither cover nor escape. Zack scanned the area, but there was nowhere left to run. The cold expanse of the bay taunted them with its indifference, the water darkening as day bled into twilight.

They were trapped.

Zack stole a glance over his shoulder to see three masked men sprinting toward them."Cover me!" he yelled, taking position behind a sturdy trash receptacle. He fired at the advancing figures, who immediately took cover.

Zack glanced over at Maya, who was now pointing fervently toward a small motorboat bobbing precariously at the dock. "There!" she shouted, her voice nearly lost in the cacophony of bullets pinging off metal and splintering wood.

Zack had no idea if the keys were in the boat or not. They would just have to find out.

Zack sprang from his makeshift cover and sprinted toward the vessel. The salty tang of sea air stung his nostrils, mingling with the acrid scent of gunpowder.

"Get in!" Maya cried. Her hand was already on the boat's ignition, fingers dancing over controls slick with evening dew. Her eyes were locked in concentration.

Zack vaulted into the boat, taking up a defensive position. His movements were fluid despite the pounding of his heart—a heart that had endured the rigors of loss and the fire of combat.

"You know how to drive this thing?" he shouted to her.

"Of course. It's not that complicated."

Turning his attention back to their attackers, Zack squeezed the trigger of his weapon, sending rounds spitting toward the shadowy figures emerging at the edge of the dock. The masked men dove for cover, buying them precious seconds.

"Come on, come on," Maya murmured, frustration seeping into her normally composed demeanor. The engine coughed and sputtered, stubbornly refusing to turn over. She pounded the dashboard with a clenched fist.

Zack glanced over his shoulder, witnessing the struggle etched across Maya's face. Doubt whispered in his ear. "I thought you said you know how to do this!"

"I do!" she snapped back, her focus entirely on the stubborn boat engine. "It's just not cooperating!"

"Damn it, Maya, we don't have time for a stubborn engine!"

Just then, the engine roared to life. A triumphant grin slashed across Maya's face as she grabbed the wheel. "Hold on!" she barked, and the boat shot away from the dock with a spine-jarring jolt.

San Francisco's bay waters churned angrily beneath them, whipped into a frenzy by the boat's powerful thrust. The darkening sky loomed overhead, streaked with the deep oranges and purples of dusk, giving way to the ominous embrace of night.

"Keep her steady!" Zack shouted over the roar of the engine as he scanned the waters behind them. It soon became apparent that their assailants had not given up: another boat sliced through the waves in hot pursuit, its outline ghostly against the dimming light.

Maya's hands gripped the wheel, knuckles white, as she navigated the treacherous dance of predator and prey. The wind whipped her hair wildly around her face, but her eyes remained steely, fixed on the path ahead.

The choppy waters threw them around, but Zack felt alive in the tumult, his instincts sharp as a blade. Each wave they crested was a challenge met, each maneuver a defiance of the odds stacked so heavily against them.

"Left! Take a hard left!" he instructed, spotting a narrow inlet that could buy them some time. Without hesitation, Maya wrenched the wheel, and the boat careened dangerously to the side, nearly tossing Zack overboard. He clung on, his muscles straining against the centrifugal force.

They shot through the inlet, the encroaching walls of rock rising like sentinels on either side. For a moment, there was silence save for the sound of their ragged breaths and the engine's relentless hum. But then, the telltale growl of their pursuer's engine rumbled ominously behind them. They were not out of danger yet.

"Keep going," Zack said. "We'll just have to outrun them."

Maya nodded in grim determination, her eyes locked onto the narrow channel that lay ahead. She pushed the throttle to its limit, the small boat leaping forward with renewed fervor. Above them, seagulls cawed a haunting melody, their silhouettes dark against the rapidly darkening sky.

Glancing back, Zack saw their pursuers bearing down upon them. Like a predator driven by raw primal instinct, they were relentless—each near miss or temporary setback only seemed to fuel their resolve.

Maya, however, was more than up to the task. She steered them through a labyrinth of inlets, her hands steady on the wheel despite the tremors that shook their bodies. The salt-laden fog rolled in thick waves, masking the boat and granting them a cloak of invisibility against their pursuers.

"Where did you learn to navigate like this?" Zack asked, his voice edged with admiration and surprise.

"Spent summers here with my dad," Maya replied without taking her eyes off the water ahead. "He loved sailing—taught me everything about these waters. Currents, hidden shoals, how the fog behaves."

As she spoke, Zack glimpsed a side of Maya he hadn't seen before: a daughter shaped by cherished memories, a woman defined by more than just her badge and gun.

"Your old man would be proud," Zack said, and meant it. He watched the deft way she dodged a half-submerged log, the confident tilt of her head as she assessed their path. Her knowledge was their lifeline, and Zack found himself relying on her expertise as much as she relied on his protection.

A dock emerged from the gloom. Zack glanced over his shoulder, searching the fog for any sign of their pursuers, but he saw no one.

Had they really lost them? Or was that wishful thinking?

The boat's hull scraped against the timeworn dock, its wooden planks slick with seaweed and brine. Zack hopped out first, extending a hand to help Maya onto the rough surface. Their footfalls were silent as they moved away from the vessel.

"Come on," Maya said. "This way."

Maya led them through a maze of crates and ropes. They emerged onto a crowded boardwalk, merging with the flow of people who thronged the area, oblivious to the life-and-death drama that had played out only moments before. It was surreal, the normalcy of it all, the innocent laughter and chatter that filled the air.

"There's an FBI safe house not far from here," Maya murmured, keeping her voice low as they weaved through the crowd. "It'll give us a chance to catch our breath and reassess."

Zack nodded, warming to this plan.

As they made their way through the crowd, however, a prickle of unease traveled down his spine, and he reached down to feel the notepad in his pocket.

Had those masked men returned for the notepad? And if they'd been willing to kill for it...then what terrible secrets might it contain?

CHAPTER TEN

Zack surveyed the cramped interior of the FBI safe house with a critical eye.

"It's not the Ritz," he said, "but it'll do."

The air was stale with the scent of disuse, every surface coated with a fine layer of dust.

He crossed the room, kicking up a tiny storm of dust from the worn-out carpet. He ran his hand absent-mindedly along an old oak table that had seen better days, picking at a loose splinter.

In the corner of the room stood an ancient bureau, its drawers hanging crooked as if on their last breaths. Above it, a cracked mirror reflected his image back at him, distorted and vague. He dragged a finger across it, watching as the dust fell away like snowflakes.

His eyes fell on a pair of worn-out leather armchairs, their once vibrant color faded to a dull brown. He flopped down into one of them, creating a cloud of dust that sent him into a fit of sneezing.

"Make yourself comfortable," Maya said, arching an eyebrow.

Remembering why they had come here, Zack rose and approached the window, then wiped away a layer of dust with the heel of his hand. Outside, the city's pulse throbbed indifferently to their plight, but he remained vigilant, searching for the masked specters that haunted their steps.

"We lost them, Zack," Maya said.

"Yeah, well, I'll believe it when I see it."

She shrugged. "I'm going to take a look around, make sure everything is secure."

Zack nodded and watched her go. Then, remembering Riley, he pulled out his phone to call her.

"Agent Carter," she said.

"Riley, it's Zack." He spoke in hushed tones as Maya kept her watchful gaze on the opposite end of the room.

"Talk to me," came the crisp response.

"We hit a wall at Angela's place. Got ambushed by some heavies in masks," Zack said, his mind replaying the gunfire, the narrow escape.

"But I found something—Angela's notebook. It's coded, but it might hold answers."

"Damn, Zack. You two okay?" There was a sharp edge of urgency in Riley's voice.

"Been better, but we'll manage. I need you to run a deep background check on Angela's associates, anyone who knew about her work. Can you do that?"

"Already on it," Riley assured him, and Zack could almost picture her, brow furrowed in concentration as she worked her contacts and databases.

"What about the power plant? Find anything new?"

Riley's voice, edged with frustration, crackled through the speaker. "No dice at Montrose. I've grilled every technician and executive who'll talk—it's like hitting a brick wall. They're either clueless, or they're masters of deception."

"Keep pushing, Riley. Someone knows something," Zack replied, his gaze never leaving the darkened streets below the safe house window. He imagined the power plant's silent turbines, the smoking ruins.

"Will do," Riley said, then paused. "Where are you now?"

"At a safe house. We'll be alright here."

"Just don't let down your guard, okay? They could still be after you."

"I never do," Zack said with a grim smile.

Riley grunted. "And for once, I'm grateful for that."

Zack hung up, pocketing the phone with a sense of foreboding. Riley, despite her uncanny ability to read between the lines, hadn't cracked the staff at Montrose yet, but if anyone could, it was her. She'd peel back their layers one by one until she found the truth, however well-hidden.

He turned from the window, feeling the weight of responsibility settle on his shoulders like an old, familiar cloak. Just then, Maya walked back into the room. "Doors and windows are all locked," she said.

"Good." Zack nodded, putting his thoughts together. "I think it's time we took another look at that notebook."

"Let's go sit down, then," Maya said, gesturing toward a doorway. Zack followed her into a living room, where they both sat down at a worn wooden table. Zack dug the notebook from his pocket and set it on the table. Its pages were riddled with inscrutable symbols and equations that seemed more akin to an ancient tome than a scientist's journal.

"Looks like some sort of substitution cipher," Maya observed, her finger tracing the looping scrawls. "But it's mixed with scientific notation. It's...unique."

"Angela was working on something. Something those thugs were ready to kill us to learn more about. If we can crack this, we might just be able to figure out what the hell's going on."

"But where do we start?"

Zack began to leaf through the notebook, searching for anything that stood out. Most of the information was encrypted, but he spotted a single word written in a tiny, neat script.

Montrose, the name of the power plant where the meltdown had occurred.

Zack's heartbeat kicked up a notch. "That can't be a coincidence," he said. The word seemed to pulse with significance, and Zack's mind whirred as he connected the dots.

Maya leaned in closer, her brow furrowed. "The power plant sabotage... You think Angela's project was related?"

"Has to be," Zack replied, his gaze locked on the page. "She visited Montrose – we know that from speaking with the Head of Personnel over there – and she was probably working on something for the plant from afar. Maybe some kind of new reactor technology?"

"And that's why she was taken," Maya murmured. "Because of her connection to the plant."

"It sure looks that way."

Neither of them spoke for a moment. Zack sensed an unspoken question hanging over them: Was Angela still alive? Had her kidnappers taken her to get something from her, or simply to execute her—perhaps because she knew too much?

"Here." Maya tapped on a margin filled with jumbled letters. "This isn't just gibberish. Look at the repetition of certain letters. It could be a cipher."

"Good catch," Zack said, the corner of his mouth lifting in a rare smile. He appreciated her sharp eye. Together, they began to sift through the symbols, translating them into something coherent, something actionable.

As they worked, the world outside faded away. The only sounds were the soft rustle of pages turning and whispered conjectures. Time stretched and bent, becoming irrelevant. Zack's every synapse fired as he absorbed the information, letting it simmer in the cauldron of his brain.

Zack's interior monologue grew increasingly frantic as he searched for a breakthrough. Angela's life could very well depend on their success here. And while the burden was heavy, his resolve was unyielding.

"Anything that mentions a location, people she met, times she was out of sight," Zack said, his mind ticking over each detail like a master clockmaker ensuring every gear was in place.

"Working on it," Maya replied, her voice a beacon of calm in the storm of their task. Her presence grounded him, reminding him that he wasn't alone in this fight.

"We'll find her, Zack," Maya said. "We'll find her."

Zack nodded. "I just hope she's still in one piece."

* * *

Zack's eyes felt like they were swimming in ink as he pored over the cryptic scrawls in Angela's notebook. Each page was a labyrinth of scientific jargon and hurried notes, the loops and lines of her handwriting undulating like waves against the shore of his mind. The room around him had faded to a mere backdrop, every shadow growing long and deep in the dim light of the single lamp that pooled its yellow glow on the table.

He didn't know how long he'd been sitting here, nor how long it had been since Maya had left the room. Thus far, all he'd been able to make out were some technical details about the operations of a nuclear plant, details that might or might not be relevant to the investigation.

"Zack." Maya's voice cut through the silence, distant yet clear. "Would you come to the kitchen for a minute?"

With a sigh that seemed to carry the weight of their predicament, Zack pushed back from the table. His muscles protested as he stood, stiff from hours of immobility. He stretched, feeling the vertebrae in his spine pop with small reliefs of tension. As he walked toward the kitchen, each footfall sounded heavy, a rhythmic thud against the bare wooden floor that echoed the pounding in his skull.

He rounded the corner and stopped, the interior monologue momentarily hushed by what lay before him.

Maya had turned the spartan space into a semblance of home. The kitchen, once cold and sterile under the harsh fluorescent lights, now glowed warmly. She had found an old tablecloth somewhere and spread it over the small table, its floral pattern blooming defiantly against the drab surroundings.

On the table sat two plates, where Maya had artfully arranged the canned goods and packets of dehydrated food that were stockpiled in the pantry. There was a can of chili, heated and spiced up with whatever seasonings she could find, next to a pile of saltine crackers neatly stacked like cards. Beside them, a medley of canned vegetables created a mosaic of color, vibrant greens and yellows and reds.

"It's not much," Maya confessed, her face softening. "But it should be better than nothing."

"Looks perfect," Zack managed to say, his stomach suddenly reminding him that he hadn't eaten since morning. As he took a seat, his gaze fell on the modest feast. Here, amidst the tension of their mission, Maya had carved out a moment of normalcy. The scent of the meal wafted to his nostrils, simple yet tantalizing.

The clink of spoons against bowls punctuated the silence between them as they began to eat. Zack savored the heat of the chili as it spread through him, fighting off the chill that had nothing to do with temperature. Across from him, Maya's gaze was thoughtful, her spoon tracing lazy circles in her bowl.

"Never thought I'd find so much comfort in canned food," Zack said, his voice low but clear in the small kitchen. He watched Maya's lips curve into a small smile, her eyes meeting his with understanding.

"Sometimes it's the simple things," she replied. "You know, this is...nice. Given everything else."

'Nice' wasn't a word Zack would have associated with their current situation, yet he couldn't deny the odd sense of camaraderie it fostered. "Tell me something," he said, trying to steer away from the investigation that loomed over them like a storm cloud. "What made you join the Bureau?"

"Ah, classic dinner conversation." Maya chuckled, then her expression turned introspective. "Honestly? I wanted to understand people. Understand why they do terrible things." Her eyes darkened with the shadows of memories he knew better than to pry into. "And maybe stop them before they can hurt others. What about you? Why'd you join the DNS?"

"Family tradition," Zack said, the words feeling heavier than they should. "My father was military. He believed in serving, protecting..." His throat tightened at the memory of his father's firm hand on his shoulder, the pride in his eyes that now shone only in Zack's recollections. "I guess I took up the mantle in my own way."

"Sounds like he was a good man."

"Best I ever knew." Zack looked down, stirring his chili. The silence stretched again, but it was softer now, less charged.

"Your turn for an anecdote," Maya prodded gently, and Zack found himself reaching back for lighter memories.

"Alright. First field assignment, I'm tailing this guy suspected of arms dealing. I follow him into a pet store, of all places." A snort of laughter escaped him. "End up accidentally releasing a bunch of parakeets during a scuffle. Feathers everywhere. Suspect got away, but I caught him two days later."

Maya's laughter joined his, bright and unexpected, washing away some of the grime of fear and uncertainty. For a moment, they were just two people sharing a meal and stories, not agents entangled in a web of danger and conspiracy.

They both fell silent.

"What about you?" Zack asked. "Any funny field stories?"

Maya's mirthful eyes sparkled under the dim kitchen light. "Oh, I've had a few run-ins with unexpected wildlife too," she began, her voice a soft thrum of warmth in the quiet room. "First assignment out of training, I'm assigned to a surveillance team in rural Montana. We're tracking this man suspected of running an illegal poaching ring. We're following him through this dense forest at night—it's pitch black except for our night vision goggles."

"And then, out of nowhere, the suspect starts scrambling up a tree. We all think we've blown our cover, that he spotted us. Turned out the poor guy was fleeing from a skunk that had wandered into his path. The smell was...unforgettable."

Zack chuckled, shaking his head as he tried to picture the scene Maya had painted. "So, what happened next?"

"We waited until dawn," Maya said with a sheepish smile. Her eyebrows rose as she continued, "Well, when the skunk finally moved on, we found our suspect passed out from fear in the branches. Took us a good hour to convince him to come down. We all stank for days, but hey, we got our man."

Zack chuckled again and leaned back, staring at his empty bowl. A breeze pressed against the house, causing the frame to creak, and Zack glanced out the window, noticing how dark it had gotten. It had to be around midnight.

Maya stifled a yawn. "I think I'm going to hit the hay," she said, rising. "There are two bedrooms upstairs. You can have the one on the right."

"What, I don't get to choose?"

"Not unless you want the one with mauve bedding."

"Oh." Zack recoiled, a shudder rippling through him. "Mauve? No, thank you." He stood up and stretched, feeling the knots in his back and neck loosening. His half-hearted attempt at humor was rewarded by a wisp of a smile from Maya.

She started clearing the table, her movements practiced and graceful. It was oddly soothing to watch. Zack moved to help her, but she waved him away. "I've got this," she said. "Get some sleep."

He nodded and added his own soft, murmured thanks for the meal. Then he trudged up the stairs and toward the right-hand bedroom, leaving Maya alone in the kitchen, which still hummed with life and warmth.

The bedroom was small, lit by a shaded lamp perched on a wooden chest. A bed nestled against the wall and a chair positioned near the window comprised its simple furnishings.

Closing his door, Zack moved mechanically through the motions of preparing for bed, though he doubted sleep would come easily. He brushed his teeth over a chipped sink, the mirror above it spotted and vague, as if unwilling to show a true reflection. He splashed water on his face and stared at the man looking back at him—tired lines etched deeper tonight, a shadow of stubble across his jaw.

Finally, drawn by an impulse he couldn't name, Zack approached the window and peered out. The city beyond lay sprawled like a living organism, lights pulsing along its veins of streets and highways. Up here, in the relative safety of elevation, it seemed peaceful, almost idyllic. But Zack knew better. Somewhere out there, danger lurked, coiled tight and ready to strike.

And Angela's fate – as well, perhaps, as the fate of countless others – hinged on the clues they could extract from that notebook.

CHAPTER ELEVEN

The morning light seeped through the blinds, casting a pattern of stripes across the room where Zack sat hunched over his laptop, a fortress of crumpled papers and empty coffee cups surrounding him like the aftermath of a bureaucratic battle. His fingers danced across the keyboard with mechanical precision, decrypting data from the notebook salvaged from Angela Horowitz's home, most of which he had already typed up. The screen flickered with strings of text as he peeled back the layers of coded information, each keystroke potentially bringing him closer to the missing physicist.

"Find anything?" Maya's voice cut through the silence as she joined him. Her eyes, sharp with analytical prowess, focused on the deciphered data scrolling down the screen.

"Bits and pieces," Zack muttered, his mind churning with theories and calculations. "Coordinates, names, dates of different projects—all scattered. It's like piecing together a shattered mirror."

"Let me help." Maya leaned in. Their shoulders brushed subtly, an inadvertent touch in the intimacy of their shared mission.

"I doubt you're going to find much," Zack said. "I've been at this for a few hours already."

She raised an eyebrow. "You don't believe in sleep, do you?"

He shrugged one shoulder. "I'll sleep when I'm dead."

"Or when you solve this case, whichever comes first." Maya's tone was teasing, but underscored with a hint of concern. Zack felt her studying him from the corners of her eyes.

He cracked a smile at her remark, his fingers never ceasing their relentless dance on the keyboard. "If it means finding Angela Horowitz..."

Maya nodded, her eyelashes casting long shadows across her high cheekbones as she frowned at the laptop screen in concentration. Then suddenly she straightened. "Look at that," she said, pointing to a string of numbers that seemed unremarkable to the untrained eye.

"I just decrypted those," Zack said. "As far as what they mean, though—"

"They could be coordinates—latitude and longitude."

Zack's pulse quickened. Of course.

"Why didn't I think of that?" he murmured.

"Sleep deprivation, maybe?"

He rolled his eyes at her. Then, wasting no time, he ran the numbers through a mapping software, and a satellite image of a mansion perched on the edge of the Hollywood Hills materialized on the screen. Elegant and imposing, the property clung to the cliffs like a modern-day fortress, its terraces overlooking the sprawling city below.

"Looks like our best lead yet," Zack said, though his gut tightened at the thought of Angela in the clutches of unknown captors within those walls. "Assuming those numbers really are latitude and longitude."

"Time for recon then?" Maya asked, her tone suggesting readiness for action.

"First, we need a plan." Zack's fingers paused above the keyboard as he considered the challenges of infiltrating such a location. It would require stealth, precision, and a thorough understanding of what they were up against.

He immersed himself in research, scouring public records and satellite imagery for any advantage. He memorized every entrance, every blind spot, internalizing the layout until the blueprint was etched in his mind.

"The best way to approach the house would be from the wooded hills back here," Zack said, tracing a line on the satellite image with his index finger. "There's cover in the foliage, and it seems to be outside the security cameras' line of sight."

Maya nodded, studying the screen closely. "Do we have any idea what kind of security system they're working with inside?"

"Not sure," Zack admitted, pulling up another page of research. "Public records indicate a top-grade system was installed five years ago, but there's no way to know if it's been updated since."

Maya sighed, pinching the bridge of her nose. "This is risky. If we're discovered..."

"I know," Zack cut in, giving her a stern look. "But it's a risk we have to take if we want to find Angela."

She exhaled slowly, rolling her shoulders back as she straightened up. "Alright then. What's our game plan?"

"*Our* game plan," Zack said, thinking on his feet, "is that I go in and you keep watch from a distance."

"Nuh-uh." Maya shook her head firmly. "No way."

"If we both go in, we'll both be blind."

"Blindness is better than helplessness," Maya said. She locked her gaze with Zack's, the resolve in her eyes matching his own. "I'm not letting you walk into potentially hostile territory alone."

Zack leaned back in his chair, the squeak of its springs protesting softly around the room as he regarded her with a thoughtful stare. Her determination was admirable, formidable even. It didn't change his plans, though.

"And I'm not letting you get killed in there," he said. "I don't want your blood on my hands."

She crossed her arms. "You don't think I can handle myself?"

"I know you can handle yourself," Zack said, holding her gaze steadily. "But there are too many unknowns; we can't predict what they might have in there." He sighed, his tone softening. "Besides, I need someone to keep watch and tell me what's going on around me. I need you, Maya."

She stared at him, clearly not liking this plan.

"Fine," she muttered eventually, her gaze breaking from his to survey the detailed map sprawled across the screen. "But I want reliable comms at all times."

his pocket and pulling out a set of high-tech earpieces—small, discreet coils of wire that could be molded to fit any ear. They were designed for stealth operations, ensuring a clear line of communication without risking discovery.

Maya hesitated for a moment before taking one, her fingers brushing lightly against his as she did.

"Let's get to work then," she said, pocketing her earpiece. "If Ms. Horowitz is in there...there's no telling what she could be going through right now."

* * *

Zack approached the mansion under the disguise of the mid-morning haze, every sense attuned to his environment. The lush greenery surrounding the property provided ample cover, enabling Zack to move closer without detection. The armed men patrolling the perimeter wore tactical gear that suggested military training, their movements disciplined and methodical.

"Check, check," Maya said, her voice filling Zack's ear. "Can you hear me?" She was nearby, positioned in a concealed spot among the foliage higher up on the hillside, armed with her tech and a bird's-eye view of the mansion.

"Loud and clear," he replied quietly, scanning through the bushes for any hidden security cameras. He had to duck low as one of the guards walked by, his boots crunching over dry leaves.

"Two guards at the front entrance," Maya reported. "Another patrolling the back terrace."

"Roger that," Zack murmured, creeping closer to the mansion. Through a gap in the verdant landscaping, he saw a state-of-the-art security camera nestled above a side door. He couldn't risk being seen.

"Any indication of Angela?" Zack asked, his heart pounding against his ribcage.

"Not yet," Maya admitted, her voice thick with worry. "I'm hacking into their security feeds now."

While she worked her magic from afar, Zack made his way toward the back of the mansion. The quiet chirping of birds masked the sound of his movements, the soft crunch of leaves underfoot. The mansion loomed overhead, its grandeur intimidating against the backdrop of a clear morning sky.

"Done," Maya's voice crackled in his ear. "I've got visual on most of the rooms now."

"And Angela?" Zack asked, peering from behind a large oak at the back entrance.

of her yet. I'll keep looking."

As Zack reached the side entrance he had scouted earlier, he paused to assess the situation. A keypad lock – no doubt with a code that changed regularly – guarded the door.

Zack cursed softly. "I've got a keypad here," he whispered to Maya. "Think you can hack it?"

"There's no manual override option," she noted, her tone grim. "Give me a moment."

As Maya worked, Zack kept his eyes trained on the mansion. His heart pounded like a drum in his chest, each beat echoing the precious seconds that were ticking away. In his mind, he replayed his contingency plans, a list of escape routes burning bright and clear.

"Got it," Maya finally announced, the relief palpable in her voice. "The code is 4962."

Zack quickly punched in the numbers. The lock beeped once, and he sighed in relief as it disengaged, letting him into the mansion.

"How in the world did you do that?" he asked.

"A good magician never reveals her secrets," Maya replied, a playful lilt to her voice despite the situation. "You have five minutes before the code resets. Move."

Stealthily, Zack slipped through the door and moved into an opulent hallway decked with Renaissance paintings and ornate chandeliers. The door clicked shut behind him, a haunting sound in the hushed silence of the mansion.

Zack's eyes, adjusted to the dim light, scanned for any signs of movement—a whisker's twitch would betray a presence to his honed senses.

In the periphery of his vision, a hulking silhouette materialized: a guard strolling by, unaware of Zack's presence. Any moment, though, the guard might turn his head and spot Zack.

Seizing the moment, Zack lunged forward, his hand clasping over the man's mouth with the precision of a sprung trap. With a fluid motion borne of countless drills, he dragged the struggling body into an adjacent room, a repository for expensive-looking art pieces.

Zack pushed the man against a painting of a storm-tossed sea, then drew his Glock – now fitted with a suppressor – and pointed it at the man's chest. "Any loud noises," he said, "and I put one through your heart."

The man, a burly brute with a scar slashed across one cheek, nodded silently, his blue eyes wide with fear. He made no move to resist.

"Good," Zack murmured. "Now tell me: Where's Angela Horowitz?"

The man's eyes widened, confusion etching his features before they set into a mask of defiance. "Who? I don't know any Angela."

Zack fixed him with a glare, one that had wilted stronger wills than this. "Don't play games with me. Lives are at stake."

"Look, buddy, I don't know who the hell you're talking about."

"Then who are you? What are you doing here?"

"I'm just a hired gun," the man confessed, perspiration starting to bead on his forehead. "Security. Nobody told me squat—just to shoot if someone came snooping around without an invite."

Zack frowned, tightening his grip on the Glock. "I don't believe you."

"Believe what you want," the man retorted, his bravery returning in spurts. "But I don't know any Angela."

"Zack," Maya said in Zack's earpiece. "I've checked all the rooms, but I can't find her anywhere. Maybe we're wrong about this."

Zack's heart sank as doubt began to creep in. But if this had nothing to do with Angela Horowitz...then what *were* these men doing here?

Just then, he noticed a tattoo on the man's neck: a serpent coiled around a dagger, its insignia unfamiliar but reeking of clandestine affiliations. He recognized that tattoo. It was the tattoo of the Black Serpent Brotherhood, a gang involved in drug-trafficking and international arms deals.

The same gang Galen Fisher had been caught up in. A shudder ran down Zack's spine.

"Something's wrong," Maya said, sounding worried. "I've got several tangos closing in on your position. You need to get out of there—now."

"Roger that," Zack murmured, nodding.

But first, he had to ensure this rogue element wouldn't be on his trail.

"Sorry, pal," he said, not sorry at all, as he delivered a precise chop to the man's neck, sending him into unconsciousness. The man collapsed to the floor, and Zack swiftly secured him with zip ties, gagged him for good measure, and hid him behind a towering sculpture that looked like it cost more than a small country's GDP.

With a final glance at the incapacitated man, Zack hurried out of the room.

As Zak crept down the hallway, heading for the back door through which he'd entered the building, a sudden creak broke his concentration. Zack froze, his ears straining against the silence that followed. The mansion seemed to breathe—an exhale of menace.

Before he could pivot, pain exploded across the back of his skull.

Vision blurred, ears ringing, Zack staggered forward. His training kicked in, his body reacting even as his mind fought through the fog of disorientation.

Zack twisted, instinctively throwing his elbow back and feeling the jarring impact of bone on bone. A grunt, and then the clatter of a dropped weapon. His attacker was momentarily stunned, and Zack didn't waste the opportunity. He lunged, hands grappling for leverage, a knee driving up to meet resistance with unyielding force. Breath whooshed out of the assailant, and Zack shoved hard, sending the man crashing into a nearby wall.

Free once more, Zack took a moment to steady himself before dashing for the exit.

Several shouts pursued Zack as he shoved the door open and raced out. Then there was the distinct rattle of gunfire, and he hurried around the building as bullets kicked up little clouds of dust around him.

"Go, go, go!" someone shouted.

Zack sprinted, feet pounding on the cobblestone pathway, zigzagging between bursts of gunfire.

There was a boom from the hillside as Maya opened fire with her high-powered rifle. "Take the car!" she told Zack. "I'll cover you!"

"They'll hunt you down!" he answered.

"So pick me up at the road! I'll meet you there!"

There was no time to argue. Zack reached the car – a nondescript sedan chosen for its blendability rather than speed – and threw himself inside. He turned the key in the ignition, and the engine roared to life. Zack threw the vehicle into gear, tires screeching as he tore out of the driveway.

The rearview mirror flashed with the rapid approach of headlights—muscular vehicles spilling forth from the mansion. They were organized, relentless.

And now they were directly on his tail, their engines snarling like beasts unleashed.

Up ahead, Zack saw Maya pelting down the hillside. He slammed the brakes, watching in silent agony as the vehicles behind them cut the distance.

"Get in!" he shouted at her.

Maya ripped the door open and jumped inside. Zack gunned the engine even before she had a chance to close the door.

Asphalt and rubber screamed in protest as he pushed the sedan to its limits, weaving through the treacherous terrain, each twist and turn a dance with death. His hands were vice grips on the steering wheel, each tendon standing out like cable wires under his skin.

"We have to lose them!" Maya said.

"Working on it!" he answered, his eyes darting to the rearview mirror.

A bullet pinged off the car's frame. Zack veered left, narrowly avoiding collision with a wayward coyote that trotted across the road, its eyes reflecting the chaos for a split second before disappearing into the brush.

"Close call," Zack muttered to himself.

"You should watch the road, not the wildlife, Force," Maya said, but there was relief tinting her words.

"Thanks for the tip," he grumbled.

His thoughts churned as quickly as the wheels spun. If these armed men were not after Angela, then what? He needed answers, but first, he needed to survive.

The road ahead twisted up the hills, houses becoming sparse, the city lights a distant glimmer below. He pressed down harder on the accelerator, the car groaning in protest. A near-miss with an oncoming vehicle sent his heart into his throat, the sedan skittering perilously close to the guardrail.

"Damn it!" he said, regaining control just as another round of bullets spurred him forward.

"Zack, listen," Maya said. "There's a construction zone up ahead—"

"Perfect," he cut in, already formulating a plan. As the orange warning lights loomed ahead, he prepared to take a gamble.

Swerving into the construction site, tires crunching over gravel, Zack navigated the labyrinth of machinery and half-finished roads. The shadows cast by the equipment were long and disorienting, perfect for his purpose. He veered off to the side and threaded the sedan between a parked bulldozer and a mound of dirt, the proximity scraping paint off the doors with a sound like tearing fabric.

He slammed the brakes, waiting.

Two, three vehicles zipped past along the road. Zack waited, wary lest there might be a fourth. But no one else appeared.

For now, at least, they'd escaped pursuit.

"I'll call my superiors," Maya said, "and have them organize a raid. They'll search that building thoroughly, interrogate everyone they find."

If there's anyone to find by then, Zack thought.

This plan did little to appease him. They had learned nothing of Angela Horowitz's whereabouts, which meant they had only given her kidnappers more time.

Time to kill her and hide her body, maybe. Or time to use her for something else, some nefarious purpose related to the attack at Montrose.

And all Zack could do was lick his wounds and hope for a stroke of luck.

CHAPTER TWELVE

The fluorescent light above the bathroom mirror flickered erratically, casting a harsh glow on the cracked tiles and the blood smeared across the porcelain sink. Zack leaned heavily against the cool surface, feeling the sting as Maya dabbed at the wound on his head with antiseptic-soaked gauze.

"Quit moving," Maya scolded softly. "You can't go out looking like you just walked off a horror movie set."

"I'm fine." Zack's words were gruff, but he couldn't suppress the wince as she applied pressure to the cut. "It's just a scratch."

"Stubborn as a mule," she muttered. Her eyes met his in the mirror, filled with concern. "You're not immortal, Zack."

He wanted to shrug off her fussing, but every touch sent a jolt of pain lancing through his skull, dredging up memories he'd rather forget—memories of chaos, gunfire, and the smell of burning flesh. His days in the Army were like dog-eared pages in a book, allowing him to immediately flip back to them and relive them, whether he wanted to or not.

The antique bathroom clock ticked in the background, its rhythmic drone accentuating the silence that shrouded them. Zack's eyes were lost in the mirror, tracing the old scars that laced his skin, each a stark reminder of a battle fought and won. His steely-eyed reflection stared back at him, stern and unbending as he swallowed down the pain.

"Zack?" Maya's voice was distant, yet insistent. He blinked, refocusing on the woman beside him.

"Sorry," he murmured, gripping the edge of the sink tighter as if it could anchor him to the present. She didn't know just how deep his scars ran. Few did.

"Does this happen often?" Maya's tone was clinical now, but her hand hesitated over his wound.

"Does what happen?" He avoided her gaze, fixing his stare on the stained tile grout.

"The flashbacks." She said the word delicately, as though it might shatter him further.

"Only when I let my guard down."

The lie came easily, but the truth was that his nights were plagued with reliving the past, with sounds of combat ringing in his ears. By day, he armored himself with duty and resolve, but the cracks were showing. He knew it. Maya knew it.

"Zack, you need to take care of yourself," she said. "You can't just patch up the physical wounds and ignore the rest. PTSD is—"

"I know what it is. I don't need you or anyone else to tell me." He sighed, letting out his frustration. "Let's just focus on the mission, okay? We've got work to do."

Maya said nothing. She finished cleaning the wound and bandaged it in silence. As she began tidying up the medical supplies, Zack leaned against the cool porcelain of the sink, his fingers tracing the edge where it met the wall—a subconscious attempt to ground himself in the present. The sharp sting on the back of his head served as a bitter reminder of their failed mission.

"Are you absolutely certain Angela wasn't there?" he asked, squinting at Maya's reflection in the mirror. "Could we have missed something?"

"I combed through every inch of the footage," she said, a note of reservation in her voice hinting that she wasn't happy about the abrupt change in subject. "There was no sign of her. And Zack, the Black Serpent Brotherhood? Nothing they do aligns with this case. I don't see the connection."

Zack winced, not from the physical pain but from the frustration that gnawed at him. It felt like they were running out of time, and every instinct screamed at him that Angela's abduction was a pivotal piece in a puzzle far larger than they could see.

"Her notebook," he muttered, more to himself than to Maya. "The answer's got to be in her notes." His hand automatically reached into his jacket pocket, feeling the worn edges of the small leather-bound book he had retrieved from Angela's home. The key to deciphering its contents lay in his ability to focus, but focus was a luxury his mind refused to afford him right now.

"Zack," Maya interjected, her voice softening as she placed a steadying hand on his shoulder. "You need to take care of yourself first. You're no good to Angela – or anyone – if you're not well. You need to go back to D.C., get some rest. That's an order, not a suggestion."

Turning to look at her squarely, Zack saw the worry etched deeply in the furrows of her brow. "And you?" he asked. "Are you going to be on bed rest, too?"

"I've got debriefing with the higher-ups. They want a full account of what went down here. Besides, I'm not the one with the bleeding head."

"Okay," he conceded, his throat tight with reluctance. "We'll both head back."

"And you'll take it easy?"

He smiled. "Of course."

Inwardly, though, he had no intention of doing so, not while he was investigating a national crisis.

* * *

Zack Force's fingers tightened on the leather steering wheel as he guided his sedan along D.C.'s rain-slicked streets. The city was a familiar maze, each turn etched into his memory like lines on a map, but today his destination was one he'd kept hidden, even from the sharp eyes of Maya Walsh.

The building he pulled up to was unremarkable, nestled between a dry cleaner and a bakery whose sweet aromas battled the more clinical scents that seeped through Zack's rolled-down window. He checked his reflection in the rearview mirror, noting the pallor of his skin and the tightness around his eyes that spoke of nights devoid of sleep and days riddled with silent battles.

"Can't let her know," he muttered to himself, shaking off the concern Maya's voice carried, even now when she was miles away. With a deep breath, he stepped out of the car and into the steady drizzle.

Inside, the doctor's office was a clean, quiet space. The walls were a soft eggshell, adorned with prints of landscapes promising tranquility.

The receptionist was a young woman, her dark hair pulled back into a neat bun. Recognizing him, she greeted him with a soft, "Good morning, Zack." Her voice was gentle, as if she were afraid a louder sound might startle him.

"Morning, Lisa," he said with a nod. She gestured toward the waiting area, where a single patient was already seated. Out of habit, Zack chose a chair in the corner, where his back would be against the wall and he could see the entrance clearly. Sitting down, he tried to focus on the calming landscape prints but found his hand gravitating back to his pocket and the worn edges of Angela's notebook.

It seemed only a few moments before the door opened and Dr. Lynn stood there, smiling at him. Her eyes immediately crinkled with concern.

"You look like shit," she murmured to him as he left the waiting room and followed her to one of the patient rooms.

"Thanks, doc," Zack replied with a grunt, settling onto the edge of the examination table with a stiffness belying his usual agility.

Dr. Lynn studied the back of Zack's head. "What happened here?"

"Got jumped by someone. It's already been patched up."

Dr. Lynn pressed her lips together in an expression of disapproval.

"Listen, doc," he said, "all I need is a refill. All that bedside manner stuff—it's not for me, okay? I have enough people worrying about me already."

"Zack, we've talked about this," Dr. Lynn said, her eyes scanning his face as if trying to decipher the secrets he fought to keep locked away. "Your condition...it's worsening. You can't keep doing this to yourself."

"Doing my job, you mean?" Zack asked, jaw set. His hands, resting on his thighs, clenched unconsciously.

"Your job is killing you." Dr. Lynn's voice softened. "You need more than medication. You need stability, rest."

"Rest doesn't stop terrorists," Zack answered, the words leaving his lips like bullets. "Rest won't find a missing physicist."

"Neither will you if you keep pushing yourself like this."

Zack remained silent, his gaze piercing through Dr. Lynn's as he digested her warning. He knew she was right, but the thought of shirking responsibility scared him more than his worsening health.

"Okay," he muttered, breaking the silence to appease the doctor. "Okay. Just...give me something to deal with the pain, okay?"

Dr. Lynn studied him for a moment longer before sighing heavily and turning toward her desk. She pulled out a prescription pad and began writing. "Two weeks," she finally said, handing him the scribbled sheet. "If your condition doesn't improve in two weeks, you have to promise me you'll consider taking a medical leave."

Zack took the prescription, his fingers brushing against the doctor's as he did. There was a subtle tremor in his grasp, invisible to the untrained eye but a sign of weakness he couldn't deny. He swallowed hard, nodded. "Two weeks," he echoed.

The cool air nipped at Zack's skin as he stepped onto the sidewalk, the numbness of his mind contrasting sharply with the sting on the back of his head. A dull throb pulsed beneath the bandage a constant reminder of his recent encounter with danger – and a reminder that Angela was still missing, her fate uncertain.

He rolled his shoulders, trying to dispel the tension and the all-too-familiar itch for action.

His hand was reaching for the car door – his next stop was the pharmacy – when the shrill ring of his phone sliced through the relative silence of the street.

Zack glanced at the screen: Director Elizabeth Murdock. Liz. He pressed the phone against his ear, steeling himself.

"Force," he answered, voice clipped.

"Zack." Liz's tone was businesslike but carried an undercurrent of concern. "The FBI made a move on the Black Serpent Brotherhood. They raided the mansion you infiltrated."

"Good," Zack replied tersely. "Did they find anything?"

"No signs of Angela, but they did manage to capture one of the gang members. He might know something about her."

Assuming she was ever there at all, Zack thought.

"Listen, I heard about your injury," Liz continued, her words slowing as if to emphasize her concern. "You're not invincible, you know."

"Scratches come with the territory," Zack said as he started the car. "I'm fine."

"Be that as it may, Zack, if you're not more careful, I'll have no choice but to take you off this case." Liz's warning rang with authority, each word a hammer driving home the severity of her statement.

"Can't do that," Zack countered, his jaw setting. "You need me."

"Damn it, Zack, I don't want something happening to you." Her voice softened, a rare moment of vulnerability from the hardened director.

"Something's always happening," Zack said as he pulled out of the parking lot. "It's the job."

"Your father wouldn't want this for you," Liz murmured, invoking a name that never failed to tighten Zack's chest.

"Respectfully, director, my father taught me to finish what I start." The words were a shield, deflecting the ghosts of the past and present. "Angela's out there somewhere. I find her, we stop another attack. That's what matters."

Liz was silent for a beat, and Zack knew she was weighing her next words carefully. Finally, she spoke again, her tone resolute. "Alright. But watch your six, Zack. I won't lose another Force on my watch."

"Understood," Zack said, though he had no intention of stepping back, not when answers were within reach, not when duty called with such ferocity. "Anything else?"

"Stay sharp. We'll talk soon." With that, the line went dead.

Why does everyone think I need to be coddled? he thought. *Don't they understand what's at stake here?*

The city blurred past Zack's window, a maelstrom of gray and steel that held no interest for him. As he maneuvered his car through the traffic, he realized he needed a fresh perspective on the case, a voice of reason who could help him figure out where to turn next.

While waiting at a red light, he reached for the phone on the passenger seat, fingers tapping the screen to life. The contact list rolled under his thumb until it stopped on a name that was both a lifeline from the past and a possible key to unlocking the future: Colonel Robert Graves.

"Graves," the voice crackled over the line, as sturdy and unyielding as the man himself.

"Rob, it's Zack." There was no need for pleasantries; their bond cut through formalities like a knife through butter.

"Force. To what do I owe the honor?"

"Need your insight," Zack said, navigating around a pothole. "On a case. It's...complicated."

"Complicated's my middle name. How about we discuss this over coffee?"

"Works for me," Zack agreed, relief threading through his voice.

"Java Joe's. Thirty minutes."

"See you there."

As he ended the call, Zack's eyes caught his reflection in the rearview mirror—a pale face, drawn tight with determination and shadowed by the memories that stalked him relentlessly. He shook his head slightly, banishing unwelcome ghosts back into the recesses of his mind.

* * *

Java Joe's was an old haunt, a place steeped in the aroma of roasted beans and the murmur of quiet conversations. As Zack entered, the bell above the door announced his arrival with a cheerful jingle. Graves was already seated in the far corner, a steaming mug cupped in his large hands.

"Zack." Graves stood, clasping Zack's hand in a firm shake that spoke volumes of their shared history.

"Rob." Zack slid into the booth, the worn vinyl creaking under his weight.

"Black coffee?" Graves gestured at the waitress who hovered nearby.

"Make it two," Zack replied.

"Zack, you look like hell," Graves said bluntly. "I heard about the plant sabotage, the missing physicist. I didn't realize what a toll it was taking on you, though."

"Occupational hazards," Zack quipped, but the smile didn't reach his eyes.

"Your father wouldn't want this for you. The PTSD..."

"Is under control," Zack interjected, his jaw tightening. He wasn't here to have his resolve questioned. "I manage."

"Because managing is what Forces do, right?" Graves' voice was softer now, concern etched into the lines of his weathered face.

"Right." Zack's gaze drifted to the window, where the world moved on, oblivious to the dangers lurking within it.

The waitress arrived with the coffee. Zack took his and wrapped his hand around the warm ceramic, its surface as gritty and worn as the man sitting across from him. The diner hummed with the low murmur of patrons and the clink of silverware on plates, a symphony of normalcy that seemed so out of place to him now. His thumb rubbed a chip on the rim, a flawed guardian against the heat—much like he guarded secrets against the daylight world.

"So," Graves said, "where do things stand with the investigation?"

"They stand still," Zack said. "Which is the problem. I think the Plantrose attack was an inside job, but I can't prove it. We found a device that appears to have been used by the saboteurs, but we haven't been able to trace its origins. And Ms. Horowitz—" He shook his head, his lips pressed together in a thin line. "She's vanished like a puff of smoke in the wind."

Graves studied him thoughtfully. "Well, a problem can't be solved if you only think in one direction," Graves said, taking a slow sip of his coffee. He set the cup down and looked at Zack with keen eyes that had seen more than their fair share of crime scenes. "You need to widen the net. Consider possibilities that seem far-fetched or even impossible."

Zack listened, his sharp gaze never leaving Graves.

"The device," Graves continued, briefly flicking his attention to the ceramic mug between his hands. "That seems like your best lead. You said you've had it thoroughly analyzed?"

"Yes. We—" He paused, thinking. Was it possible Angela had something to do with the device? She had visited Montrose, after all. What if she hadn't actually been kidnapped, but instead the scene at her house had been staged? What if she was actually working with the people who had triggered the meltdown?

Just then, Zack's phone vibrated in his pocket, a sudden intrusion that made his pulse jump. He fished it out, glancing at the caller ID.

Maya.

Excusing himself with a tilt of his head, he rose and stepped away, pressing the phone to his ear.

"Maya, tell me you have good news."

"Zack, it's about the Brotherhood member we nabbed," she said, her voice edged with tension.

"What is it? Did you learn anything from him?"

"No. He's dead, Zack—committed suicide in his cell an hour ago."

The words hit Zack like a physical blow. "He must've known something he couldn't risk sharing," he murmured.

"Something so important," Maya added, "that he needed to keep it from us at all cost—even the cost of his own life."

CHAPTER THIRTEEN

Zack stood motionless, his gaze fixed on the drab interior of the holding cell at FBI headquarters, where a man had taken his own life just a few hours ago. The air was thick with the scent of industrial cleaner and a metallic tang that might have been blood or fear—or both.

Maya Walsh, a few paces away, clutched a nondescript brown bag containing the dead man's personal items.

"Found him at 0600," the guard, a burly man with tired eyes, reported. "He was hunched over, no signs of struggle."

"Thank you," Zack said, barely acknowledging the guard as he stepped into the cell. The small space felt even more confined now, shadows clinging to the corners where the overhead lights didn't reach. He scanned the room, reconstructing the final moments within these walls. His eyes traced the path from the cot's rumpled sheets to the stainless-steel sink, then to the makeshift noose fashioned from torn fabric.

"Did we get anything from him before this?" Zack asked, his voice steady despite the grim tableau before him.

"Only a few minutes of questioning," Maya replied. "He refused to talk. Just sat there, staring blankly ahead."

"Defiant till the end," Zack mused. This wasn't just a desperate act of self-destruction—it was a statement about the importance of the information they were after.

"Could have provided answers. Now he's taken them to the grave," Zack muttered under his breath, frustration lining his face. "Any signs he was coerced, or that someone came in here with him?"

Maya shook her head. "I checked the cameras. He was alone."

Zack turned to the bag in Maya's hand. "Let's see what he left behind," he said, holding his hand out for the bag. His fingers brushed against Maya's briefly as she passed it to him, a fleeting connection in the midst of violence and uncertainty.

Zack opened the bag and began sifting through its contents: a watch, a crumpled pack of cigarettes, a few coins. His fingers paused as they wrapped around a wallet, the leather aged and creased from use.

"I'm assuming you've already checked it out?" he asked.

Maya nodded.

Zack unfolded the wallet carefully, feeling the tangible presence of a life now extinguished. The ID card displayed a photo of a man with a hollow gaze, the name 'David Riker' embossed beneath it. Zack studied the face, committing every line to memory.

"David Riker," he murmured, almost to himself, before looking up at Maya. "Well, at least we can put a name to a face."

"Except it's not his real name," Maya replied. "We ran his prints. His real name is Leo Gratz."

"Leo Gratz," Zack repeated. He pondered the implications, flipping through the wallet for any more inconsistencies.

"Gratz wasn't just some small-time thug trying to ride the coattails of the Brotherhood, either," Maya continued. Her arms were crossed, her posture professional yet alert.

"Then who was he?" Zack asked.

"A CIA agent," Maya said, the word dropping like a stone into still water. "Rogue. His last known assignment was deep cover work in Eastern Europe."

"A CIA agent..." Zack echoed, letting the revelation sink in. A rogue government agent masquerading as a gang member—this complicated things. And confused them, too.

"Do we know anything about what he was involved in?" he asked. "Any idea why he was at that mansion?"

Maya shook her head. "None."

"Whatever plan he was a part of, I have a feeling it doesn't end with Montrose or Angela Horowitz," Zack said, conviction steeling his voice.

He flipped the wallet open again, his fingers methodically working through its contents as carefully as if they were the components of a bomb. The leather was worn at the edges, creased with the habitual opening and closing by hands that would never see sunlight again. He paused at a plastic card, its blue and yellow hues glaringly out of place among the dull grays and browns.

A New York Metro card.

"Maya," Zack asked, "where was this guy's legal residence?"

"California," she replied without missing a beat, her gaze fixed on him. "Never lived in New York—we checked."

"Then what's he doing with a Metro card?" Zack murmured more to himself than to Maya, flipping the card between his fingers. It was new, hardly used—the magnetic strip barely scratched. His mind started churning, piecing together a jigsaw puzzle with too many missing pieces. "He's from California, but carries a Metro card..."

"Zack?" Maya asked. "What are you thinking?"

"New York," he said abruptly, eyes aflame with the spark of realization. "This could mean another attack. The Metro...it's a perfect target: dense crowds, contained environment. We need to get to New York now."

"Let's not jump to conclusions," Maya said. "There are a thousand reasons why he might've gotten a Metro card."

"Maya, we're not talking about a regular Joe here. This is a rogue CIA operative with ties to a notorious gang. Everything he had on his person, he had it there for a reason. We have to take this seriously."

Maya stared at him for a few moments, looking ready to argue. Then she sighed. "Okay. Let's go check it out." She packed away the remaining items swiftly. Then they left the cell.

Their footsteps clapped along the corridor as they made their way out of the building, each footfall a ticking second against the countdown in Zack's head. He drew his phone from his pocket, hitting Riley's number before they even reached the exit. Her voice was a welcome anchor in the storm of his thoughts.

"Riley, it's me. Our guy had a New York Metro card on him—unused, new. His residence is in California. I'm thinking the Metro might be the next target. I'm heading there now."

"Got it," Riley said. "There's something else. Almost everyone from the Montrose attack has been accounted for, dead or alive, but two in particular are missing: a pair of Korean nationals known to be as close as brothers. There's a chance they weren't just plant workers. They could've been government agents, maybe North Korea."

"Damn it." Zack exhaled, tension coiling within him like a spring. "Keep digging and stay safe. Update me the moment you have anything."

"Will do. Be careful, Zack."

"Always am," he replied, though the promise felt as fragile as a paper shield.

The FBI parking garage felt like a mausoleum as Zack and Maya approached the government-issued sedan. Fluorescent lights hummed faintly overhead, casting long shadows across the concrete that seemed to stretch and reach for them as they walked. The air was heavy with exhaust fumes and the lingering tension from the discovery at the holding cells.

"Zack." Maya's voice broke the silence, her tone carrying a rare softness that made him pause by the car door. "I think I need to stay here in D.C."

He turned to face her, noticing for the first time the strain around her eyes, the determined set of her jaw. Even in the sterile light, there was an undeniable connection binding them—two soldiers in a war against the clock.

"Are you sure? I could really use you in New York." His hand found the cold metal of the car handle but didn't pull.

"Someone has to follow up on Angela Horowitz's trail here," she replied, her fingers brushing against the leather bag that held the dead man's belongings. "And I need to see this through."

He nodded, understanding her resolve. Yet he couldn't ignore the reluctant pull in his chest, a silent admission of how much he'd come to rely on her insight, even in such a short time.

"Then be careful, Maya," he said earnestly, the words thick with unspoken sentiment. "This is bigger than we thought, and it's not over yet."

"Same to you, Zack. Remember, we're just a call away." She offered a tight smile, a brave front amid the brewing storm.

For a moment, neither moved, their shared goodbye hanging between them—a quiet promise neither knew if they could keep. Finally, Zack opened the car door and slid behind the wheel.

"Take care of D.C. for me," he murmured, starting the engine.

"Will do," Maya replied, stepping back as the car pulled away. In the rearview mirror, he saw her figure diminish, but the imprint of her presence lingered—a silent ally in the shadows.

* * *

Zack watched the other passengers with envy, most of whom were either sleeping or staring at screens. *Must be nice to take a mental vacation,* he thought. He knew all too well how futile it would be to attempt to do the same.

Recalling the prescription he'd filled earlier, he pulled out a pill bottle, unscrewed the cap, and slipped a pair of pills into the palm of his hand. He downed them with a swallow of water, then leaned back against his seat. He studied the in-flight safety card tucked into the seat pocket in front of him, tracing the pictures with his eyes as he forced his mind to slow down. To wait.

He thought of how worried everyone seemed to be about him, and he wondered if they were right to worry. Was he pushing himself too hard? He had always believed that he could push himself harder, further, and that the only limitations he knew were in his mind.

But what if that was the very problem—that his limitations were in his mind? He had seen enough fellow veterans go into a tailspin, their PTSD spiraling out of control as the relentless pursuit of their missions slowly consumed them. Had he become one of those men? Was he merely a walking ghost, an echo of his former self?

Deep down, Zack had always considered himself different from his comrades. He had seen the same horrors, walked on the same blood-soaked grounds, but he had always been able to distance himself from the atrocities. To compartmentalize. But the lines now seemed fuzzier than ever. The nightmares were growing more frequent. And vivid. On some nights, they were so real that he awoke sweaty and disoriented, gasping for breath. His pillow soaked with cold sweat, evidence of the internal struggle he was constantly fighting.

You gotta keep your mind occupied, he told himself, shaking his head as if that would dispel his doubts and fears. He pulled up his phone and began researching everything he could find about New York City's nuclear facilities, searching for anything that suggested a correlation with Montrose or Dr. Horowitz.

As the plane sliced through the sky, however, Zack found himself increasingly unable to separate the past from the present, and as his eyes grew blurry and he leaned his head back against the seat, his ears were filled not with the hum of the plane or the murmurs of quiet conversation, but with shouts.

The shouts of his dying comrades.

CHAPTER FOURTEEN

Zack felt a pang of unease as he stood before Leo Gratz's apartment in the Bronx, worried that this might turn out to be just another dead end.

You can't think that way, he told himself. *Control what you can control, and let the chips fall where they may.*

It was a nondescript building, shabby with years of neglect, the once vibrant red brick now faded and marred by graffiti. A good hideout for a rogue agent.

Zack climbed the steps and tried the door. It was locked, glancing discreetly around to make sure no one was watching, he slipped a small lock pick from his pocket, a tool he had grown proficient in using over the years. He listened to the subtle clicks of the tumblers falling into place, music to his ears. With a slight turn of his wrist, the door gave way.

The apartment welcomed him with an air of normalcy—a couch poised for guests that would never arrive, a coffee table stacked with espionage novels that screamed irony, and photographs lining the walls, capturing smiles frozen in time. He switched on his flashlight, the beam cutting through the dimness like a promise of revelation.

Methodically, Zack scanned each room. He sifted through drawers filled with neatly folded clothes, checked under the bed for any hidden compartments, and examined bookshelves for books out of place. Nothing.

Descending into the basement, Zack felt the temperature drop significantly. This was the underbelly where secrets loved to fester. The concrete floor was cold and unwelcoming, a thin layer of dust veiling its surface.

The basement was empty, but it did not take long for Zack to discover signs that it hadn't been empty for long. There were fresh scuff marks on the concrete floor, evidence of furniture being moved around, and holes in the wooden walls indicated where objects – blueprints, maybe? – had been tacked.

"Someone spent a lot of time down here," he whispered. In one corner, behind the water heater, he discovered a mini screwdriver, the kind used for dealing with computers. And when he searched beneath the stairs, he came across a small, crumpled paper tucked against the wood as if deliberately hidden there.

He unfolded the paper, and his breathing seemed to stop of its own accord. It was a rough drawing of the very device he and Riley had discovered at Montrose.

Zack's fingers trembled ever so slightly as he keyed in the secure number for Riley. The basement's dim light flickered overhead.

"Riley," Zack said, trying not to speak too quickly in his excitement. "I'm at Gratz's place. The basement...I think they held Angela here, made her build the Montrose device."

"Shit." Riley's voice crackled through the line, tinged with disbelief. "You sure?"

"I've got a drawing of the device here in my hand. It can't be a coincidence. I just hope..." He paused, hating the thought that had just occurred to him.

"What?"

"That they still have a use for her, because if they don't..." He left the implication unsaid.

"Well, we might have something to say about that. We've intercepted coded chatter in your area, and a particular location keeps popping up. It might be where they're keeping her now."

"Give me what you've got," Zack demanded, his pulse racing.

"Coordinates point to an old automotive factory, outskirts of Queens," Riley said. "The Redhook Motor Plant. Granted, I don't know what the chatter is about, so it could be anything—"

"Thanks, Riley. I'm on my way." He was already bounding up the stairs.

"Wait!" Riley cried. "I'm reaching out to local law enforcement. Just wait a few minutes and—"

"No can do," Zack said as he hurried through the apartment. "She might not have that kind of time."

Riley started to protest further, but Zack hung up, his decision made.

"Hang on, Angela," he muttered as he shoved open the outside door and stepped out.

He hurried down to his car and fired up the engine, then slammed his foot on the gas and pulled away. The engine roared to life beneath his hands, the hum of the car merging with the cacophony of the city. Zack navigated onto the street, tires screeching as he weaved between the slow-moving traffic like a predator threading through lesser beasts.

Taxi horns blared their annoyance, and pedestrians leapt back onto curbs, expressions morphing from irritation to shock. Zack's jaw was set, his eyes fixed ahead as he calculated his next move through the urban maze.

"Careful," he muttered to himself, downshifting as he approached an intersection. The light was red, but hesitation was a luxury he couldn't afford. He glanced both ways—traffic was coming, but there was a gap. Just enough. With a deep breath, he gunned the engine and shot through the crosswalk, narrowly avoiding a collision with a city bus that honked its disapproval long after he'd passed.

"Sorry," he murmured, though there was no one to hear the apology. Every near-miss was a reminder of the fine line he walked between duty and recklessness. His heart pounded in his chest, a staccato rhythm that matched the throb of the city around him.

"Come on, come on," Zack urged the vehicle, as if the steel and circuits could comprehend his desperation. The skyscrapers loomed above, indifferent observers to his solitary race against time. He swerved around a delivery truck that had decided to double park, the scrape of metal a hair's breadth away from his side mirror. He didn't flinch, didn't falter. He simply drove on, propelled by a force greater than fear.

The sky bled orange and purple as dusk settled over the city, casting long shadows that slithered across the desolate expanse of the abandoned automotive factory as it appeared in the distance. The building was a sleeping giant of rusted metal and broken windows, an eerie mausoleum of industry's past. Zack Force parked his car a block away, the thrum of its engine dying in a soft purr as he cut the ignition. He eyed the structure through the rearview mirror, his gaze sharp, calculating.

"Big place for big secrets," he muttered to himself, pulling out his Glock 19. The weight of the weapon in his hand was familiar, reassuring. He checked the magazine, a ritual of preparedness, before sliding out of the car. The cool evening air kissed his face, carrying the scent of ozone and decay.

"Hang in there, Angela," he murmured as he advanced toward the factory. "I'm coming for you."

CHAPTER FIFTEEN

Zack approached the Redhook Motor Plant under the veil of darkness, his boots silent on the clean asphalt. The old factory, once a bustling hub of industry, now played host to a different kind of activity. Armed figures patrolled the grounds or stood sentinel at windows, their bearing and movements suggesting military training.

Spotting two figures standing close together, Zack crept closer and hid behind a forklift as he listened to their conversation.

"And what if he talks?" the man asked, puffing on a cigarette. "If he rats on us, we're screwed."

"Leo won't rat on us," the second figure, a woman, said. "He could be bound and gagged in some hole, but he'll still be loyal to us."

Zack's heart tightened at the mention of Leo Gratz. Apparently, these two didn't know that Leo had already killed himself, an act that only solidified Zack's suspicions about the depths of this conspiracy.

"Leo's silence doesn't mean we're safe," the man insisted, pacing like a caged animal seeking escape from its inevitable fate. "They'll find another angle. They always do."

"Then we'll be ready for them," the woman replied.

Studying the two figures from his hiding place, Zack realized he would need to question one of them about Angela's whereabouts. The factory was far too massive for him to go blindly searching for her, not if there was another way.

Zack's gaze flitted across the cavernous space, taking in the derelict machinery and scattered debris with a tactical eye. He needed a diversion, something to separate the two figures who might hold the key to Angela's whereabouts. As if in answer, his attention settled on an aging conveyor belt laden with rusting car parts. A plan took shape.

Moving quietly, he edged toward the control panel nestled in the shadows, its buttons worn by time and neglect. A smirk touched the corner of his mouth as he pressed a sequence, the machinery groaning to life with a jolt. The conveyor belt lurched forward, sending a cascade of metal components clattering to the concrete floor. The din was thunderous in the stillness of the night.

"Go check it out!" the woman said to her companion. Zack watched as the man hesitated, then hustled toward the source of the commotion, weapon drawn.

There's a good boy, Zack thought, feeling the hunter within him sharpen.

The factory floor loomed large and desolate as the male agent disappeared into the maze of machinery. Now was the moment Zack had been waiting for. He shifted his weight, every muscle coiled and ready as his target – the female agent – stood alone, her silhouette etched against the far wall.

He closed the distance between them with the silence of a shadow, but as he neared, she spun with startling agility, her eyes flashing.

"Who are—" Her question was cut short as Zack lunged to grab her.

She countered with a swift jab, her training evident in the fluidity of her movements. Zack parried, surprised by her skill.

She tried to level her weapon at him, but he struck it out of her hand, and it went careening through the air. Then one of her fists struck his gut, and he doubled forward, grabbing at her.

"Enough!" he growled, shoving her against the cold metal of a dormant assembly robot. He slipped his gun beneath her chin, and she immediately stopped fighting. She glared at him, defiant.

"Where is Dr. Horowitz?" Zack demanded. "Is she here?"

"Even if I knew," she said, "I wouldn't tell a government stooge like you."

"Stooge?" Zack felt an absurd urge to laugh. "Listen," he said, "I don't know what kind of operation you and your little pals have going on here, but—"

His words were interrupted by the sharp crack of a gunshot. The bullet ricocheted off the metal mere inches above Zack's head.

Instinct took over as Zack let go of the agent and hurled himself behind the nearest stack of industrial tires, remnants from the factory's heyday.

"Over there!" a voice shouted, the words sharp and clear in the cavernous space.

"Flank him!" another said. "I'll keep him pinned!"

Zack knew he was outnumbered and outgunned. They were moving swiftly, tightening the net around him with military precision.

Zack clutched his weapon close to his chest, rolling away from the makeshift barricade just as bullets pummeled into the tires. He rose and bolted toward the assembly line. Bullets whistled past, each one a grim reminder of his mortality. He could smell the acrid scent of gunpowder mixed with oil and steel, a toxic perfume that filled the factory.

"Left side! Left side!" someone called out, trying to coordinate their attack.

Zack's boots pounded the gritty floor, every muscle coiled and ready to react. He ducked under a robotic arm once used for welding car doors, its dormant state belying the deadly potential it still possessed. With a practiced motion, he spun a control valve, releasing a hiss of steam into the air.

"Watch your six!" an agent yelled, momentarily disoriented by the sudden cloud billowing around them.

"Where is he?" another cried. Zack's diversion had worked. He slipped between machines like a ghost, using the noise and confusion to mask his movements.

His father had taught him long ago to use whatever resources were available to survive—to turn the environment into an ally. This factory was now his battlefield, and he would wield it as deftly as a soldier brandished his rifle.

"Spread out! He can't have gone far," a deep voice ordered.

Zack began jogging. The factory's bowels echoed with the sound of his pursuers, their voices bouncing off the high ceiling, chasing him deeper into darkness. Zack's breath came hard and fast, heart pounding against his ribs like a caged animal desperate to break free. He knew he was running out of time and options.

"Over here! I heard something!" an agent shouted from behind, their footsteps clanging on the metal platforms.

He needed to disappear, to become one with the shadows that danced along the grimy walls of the Redhook Motor Plant. As he sprinted through a narrow corridor, the stink of oil and sweat thick in the air, Zack's mind raced for a plan, any plan, that would give him the upper hand.

"Check every corner!" another voice commanded, closer now, more urgent.

Zack rounded a corner and there it was—an office, a beacon of faint light beneath a door cracked open, but guarded by an armed man whose silhouette was outlined by the dim glow from within. The man's stance was lax, unaware of the storm headed his way.

I wonder what he's guarding, Zack thought.

The guard noticed Zack at the last second, bringing up his weapon with trained precision. "Stop right there!" he shouted.

But Zack was faster. His finger squeezed the trigger before the other man could fully raise his gun, and the sharp report echoed through the factory. The guard crumpled to the ground.

"Jim? Jim, do you copy?" It was the fallen man's radio. Zack ignored it and approached the door.

With two swift kicks, the locked door gave way under the force of his boot, splintering wood adding to the cacophony of his entry. He stepped into the office, his weapon raised, only to discover a middle-aged woman tied to a chair, staring at him with wide, clover-green eyes.

"Dr. Angela Horowitz?" Zack asked.

She nodded, swallowing hard. "That's right. And who are you?"

"Zack Force, Department of National Security. I'm here to get you out." His gaze swept over the room, cataloging exits. There was a door at the back. He just hoped it wasn't a dead end.

"Thank God," Angela whispered, her voice shaking. "I didn't think anyone would come."

"Let's worry about thanks later. Can you walk?" He cut through her bindings with a pocket knife, watching her rub circulation back into her wrists.

"Yes, but where—" She started rising unsteadily to her feet.

"Later. Follow me and stay close."

The thump of heavy boots drew nearer. "They're here," Zack said, pushing Dr. Angela Horowitz toward the back door. "Move."

"It's locked," Angela said, gesturing at the padlock securing the door. "We can't—"

Zack shot the lock, which snapped apart and fell to the ground. It was a risky decision, given the chances of a ricochet, but there was no time for second-guessing.

Zack kicked the door open, and they rushed through a second office before finding themselves out in the open space of the abandoned automotive factory once again.

They moved swiftly, Angela keeping pace as they navigated through the tangled innards of the factory. Every shadow seemed to move, every noise a potential threat. Zack's senses were on high alert, his father's presence a ghostly weight on his shoulders.

"I can hear them behind us!" Angela whispered fiercely.

"Keep moving—I'll worry about them." Zack turned around and fired at a pair of agents as they rounded a corner. They retreated, ducking for cover.

"Will they ever stop?" Angela gasped as she and Zack sprinted forward.

"Not until they've got what they want," Zack replied grimly. "Or they're all dead."

They needed to get outside, needed to find their way back to Zack's vehicle. But as he and Angela neared a loading door leading out of the factory, several figures opened fire at them from behind a barricade of steel barrels. Zack grabbed Angela's arm and jerked her behind the frame of a tireless car.

Zack looked back the way they'd come and saw several more agents rushing toward them. They were surrounded.

"We can't just sit here," Angela said. "We have to do something!"

Then Zack spotted it: a sewer grate used to drain runoff from the factory floor. It was a tight fit, but they could squeeze through.

"Dr. Horowitz," he said, pointing at the grate, "we're going underground."

"Are you crazy?"

"It's a lot less crazy than staying here. Come on!"

Crouching low in the hope that none of the agents would see their escape, Zack grabbed Angela's arm and led her to the drain. Holstering his gun, he lifted the grate so she could climb down. Then he followed her down, closing the grate above him.

He descended the ladder and then paused at the bottom, listening, his nostrils full of the strange, chemical odor of the plant's runoff. Footsteps drummed overhead, passing the drain.

"That little trick won't fool them forever," Angela whispered.

"No," Zack answered, "it won't." He pulled out his flashlight and trained the beam on the tunnel ahead of them. "But with any luck, we'll be long gone by the time they figure it out."

CHAPTER SIXTEEN

Zack adjusted the blinds of the safehouse's single window, casting a lattice of shadow and sunlight across the room. The glow illuminated Angela Horowitz's pale but determined face as she sank into a threadbare armchair that had seen better days. She clutched a mug of coffee like a lifeline, steam curling up toward her bruised cheek where one of her captors had struck her. Zack felt a twinge of pity for the woman, knowing full well the terror she must have endured.

"Thank you, Agent Force," Angela murmured, her voice flecked with the remnants of fear. "I don't know what would've happened if you hadn't come for me."

"Call me Zack." His expression remained stoic despite the maelstrom of emotion churning within him. He pulled out a small digital recorder from his jacket pocket, clicked it on, and placed it on the scarred coffee table between them. "Tell me everything," he said, the words more of a gentle command than a request.

Angela took a deep breath, her fingers tightening around the ceramic. "It started with a surprise conversation with a stranger while I was buying groceries," she began, her gaze distant as if reliving the nightmare. "A man – his face was well hidden behind sunglasses and a thick beard – offered me twenty million dollars to assist on a classified project." A humorless laugh escaped her lips. "Twenty million to sell my soul."

She paused, shaking her head. "I knew something was off. I turned him down, tried to forget about it. But..." Her voice trailed off as she glanced toward the window, as though expecting masked figures to appear at any moment.

"Then they came for me." Her words were punctuated by the clink of her mug touching the table. "Masked men, armed, efficient. They burst through my door like a tempest, sweeping me away in seconds." Her eyes met Zack's, a silent plea for understanding—or perhaps forgiveness.

Zack's jaw tightened, his hand involuntarily forming a fist. "And the device?" he asked.

The mention of the device triggered a visible shudder in Angela. "They...they kept me in a basement, nothing but workbenches and equipment. They told me what to build, watched my every move. They were planning to use it to sabotage a nuclear facility."

"Montrose," Zack said, the word tasting like ash in his mouth.

"That's right." Angela's voice broke, and she wrapped her arms around herself. "They used it to trigger the meltdown. Those people, those poor innocents who died..." She choked back a sob, her eyes brimming with tears. "I never wanted this. I'm a physicist, not a terrorist."

"I know," Zack said. "You didn't have a choice." He reached over, placing a comforting hand on Angela's shoulder. "This isn't on you. It's on them."

Angela nodded, wiping her tears with the sleeve of her faded sweater as Zack withdrew his hand. "I know. Still...I can't help wondering if I should've just resisted, should've let them kill me. They told me the device was just meant to be used as a threat, a bargaining chip—never an actual weapon."

Zack's stern gaze softened at her words. He'd seen this story unfold too often, good people caught in the grisly web of immoral men. "You did what you had to, Angela," he said, his voice resolute. "You survived. And now we have a chance to make things right."

The room lapsed into silence, disturbed only by the distant hum of city traffic filtering through the window. Zack stood abruptly, pacing toward the window and gazing out onto the deserted road below.

He turned back to face Angela. "Do you think they were planning to use you again—for future attacks, I mean?"

She looked up at him, her pale face etched with fatigue and fear. "Yes," she whispered, the word wrought with certainty. "They mentioned...other projects. But I don't know any specifics—they kept me in the dark about their broader intentions."

Zack nodded, feeling the familiar clench of frustration in his gut. Her lack of knowledge was a dead end they couldn't afford. His gaze sharpened as he pressed on. "Anything you can remember could be vital. Locations, code names, anything."

Angela shook her head slowly, her tangled hair catching the light. "I'm sorry. They were meticulous about keeping things compartmentalized. I only knew what they needed me to know."

He sighed and turned off the recorder. "Thank you, Angela. You've been very helpful. Now get some rest—there's a bed in the other room. You've been through hell."

Angela nodded and, rising, gave him a tentative, grateful smile before leaving the room. After she'd gone, Zack pulled out his secure phone and dialed an encrypted frequency, contacting both Director Murdock and Riley.

The two women answered only moments apart.

"What is it, Agent Force?" Liz asked. "What have you learned from Dr. Horowitz?"

"Angela's confirmed her forced involvement in the Montrose sabotage," Zack began, pacing the length of the room as he spoke. "But that's all she knows. It's clear the terrorists have more planned, but we're blind to details."

"I'm told you refused to wait for backup," Liz said. "Don't you remember our last conversation?"

"I made a judgment call," Zack said, growing agitated. "A woman's life was at stake."

"And so is yours. You have to stop gambling with your life, Zack. You won't always get lucky."

He sighed. "I understand your concern. But with all due respect, I need you to trust me on this. I'm getting results."

There was a pause, and the silence stretched taut across the unseen miles. Finally, Liz exhaled audibly, her voice softening. "Alright. But you keep me informed every step of the way, understood?"

"Of course."

"And you keep Agent Carter in the loop."

"Naturally."

"I'll keep an eye on him," Riley said, her voice infused with protective resolve.

"Good," Liz said, though she sounded less than satisfied. "I'll let you two discuss next steps. I have to give a report—even *I* report to someone, believe it or not."

With that, Liz left the call.

"Riley," Zack said into the phone, his voice low and steady, "I've been thinking. Remember that Metro card we found in Leo Gratz's belongings? It makes sense they'd strike there. It's the pulse of the city. If they're looking to instill fear, that's where I'd hit."

"You might be right," Riley said, "but that's a vast network. Any specific lines or stations?"

Zack considered. "Well, no."

"So what makes you think they wouldn't attack another nuclear facility? Maybe they're planning to go after nuclear facilities across the country, shut down the power grid—all while spreading radiation and panic."

Zack had to admit it was an interesting theory—and viable, given the previous attack.

"Maybe," he said, scratching the stubble on his chin. "But Angela mentioned 'other projects'. Projects suggest diversity. I don't think redundancy is their style."

"Wait." Angela's voice sliced through their strategizing, unexpectedly sharp. She was standing in the doorway, a haunted look etched upon her face. "I remember something...a phrase they kept repeating. 'The heart will stop beating.'"

Zack turned, studying her face. "What heart?"

"They could be talking about the Metro," Riley said. "It's the heart of the city. And if it stops...the city stops."

"Or," Zack said, now arguing against his earlier theory, "they could be talking about the nation's heart. D.C."

Nobody spoke for several moments. Yes, it made sense that they would strike at the heart of the country where they could do the most damage.

"If that's the case," Riley said, "what's the target? The White House? Capitol Building?"

"Too many options," Zack answered. "We sweep to the major landmarks, start evacuation protocols."

"Zack," Riley interjected, her voice firm. "We can't just evacuate the entire city based on a hunch and a cryptic phrase."

"I know," he admitted, his frustration evident. "But we need to do something."

"And we will," Riley assured him. "But it's going to be meticulous work. We need to trace back every lead, identify patterns, put together a profile of these terrorists. Their target isn't random; it was chosen for a reason. We find that reason, we find the target."

A silence lingered in the room as Zack mulled over her words.

"The question is," Riley said, "how do we do that?"

Zack straightened and met her gaze, a plan taking shape in his mind. "I know just the person who can help us," he said.

CHAPTER SEVENTEEN

The air within the coffee shop was saturated with the scent of roasted beans and the low hum of whispered conversations. A gentle clattering of porcelain mugs punctuated the silence as Zack slid into a booth, his gaze fixed on Angela Horowitz, her fingers nervously twisting a napkin. Across from her and beside Zack, FBI profiler Maya Walsh had opened a small, black notebook, her pen poised.

Zack had mixed feelings about the art of profiling. Though he knew it had proven very useful in a number of cases, he preferred to rely on facts, believing that human behavior was too unpredictable to be neatly boxed into psychological profiles.

Here's to hoping Maya proves me wrong, he thought.

"Angela." Maya's voice was soothing, almost hypnotic. "I need you to tell me everything you can about the man who approached you. Think back to that day."

Angela looked up, her eyes meeting Maya's. The confidence in Maya's gaze seemed to reach out and steady Angela's nerves. She hesitated, biting her lip. "It's all so blurry," she admitted.

Maya nodded, patient. "Let's start with something simple. Was he tall or short?"

"Average height, I suppose," Angela said after a moment, her voice gaining strength. "But he stood very straight, like a soldier, maybe."

"Good, good." Maya scribbled down notes. "What about his voice? Anything distinctive?"

Angela closed her eyes, concentrating. "Deep," she murmured. "And...precise. He enunciated every word carefully."

"What about his mannerisms? Can you remember how he acted? Was he nervous, confident?"

"Confident," Angela said. "He never fidgeted, just...very sure of himself."

Zack felt a surge of admiration for Maya's technique. She was peeling away layers of uncertainty from Angela's mind with each question. He leaned forward, his elbows on the table, curious to hear where this might be leading.

"His hands," Maya continued. "Did he do anything notable with them?"

Angela's eyes snapped open. "Yes, he...he kept touching his left cufflink, almost like a habit."

"Perfect," Maya murmured, her pen dancing across the page as she recorded everything. "Was there anything he wore or carried that stood out to you? A watch, a ring?"

"Nothing," Angela said, then paused, a furrow appearing between her brows. "Wait, he had a...a sort of pin, maybe military, on his lapel. It was small, but it gleamed in the light."

A waitress arrived and poured coffees for them. The delicate clink of porcelain disturbed the silence as Zack watched Angela's hands tremble slightly around her coffee cup.

Maya leaned forward, her eyes never leaving Angela's face. "Anything else about him that you can remember? A scent or a particular way he spoke?"

Angela closed her eyes, inhaling deeply as if to dredge up the memory from the depths of her mind. Zack observed her, knowing the importance of these small fragments of recollection. They were often the keys that unlocked entire investigations.

"His voice," Angela murmured, her eyelids fluttering open. "It had an odd cadence, like...he was trying to mask an accent."

"Was it successful?" Maya prodded gently.

"Mostly, but there was something... No, it was more than that." Her brow creased in concentration, then smoothed as clarity dawned. "He sounded...well, Asian, I would say."

"Korean?" Zack asked, thinking of the two North Korean workers who had gone missing from Montrose.

Angela pressed her lips together uncertainly. "It's possible, but I can't say for sure."

Zack felt his heart rate kick up. Rising, he stepped away from the table to call Riley.

"What is it?" she asked, sounding distracted. "I'm on the other line with a friend from the CIA—filling them in so we can pool resources."

"I just need you to find someone for me," he said. "Angela was contacted by someone who may have been North Korean. He was average height, probably ex-military, thick beard and sunglasses. Can you cross-reference the two North Koreans missing from Montrose, see if they have any associates who fit that description?"

"Got it," Riley said. "I'll get back to you as soon as I've got something."

"Thanks, Riley."

Zack returned to the table and settled back into the booth seat. Maya was still gently probing Angela, careful not to overwhelm her.

"Was there anything else that stood out about this man? Any other distinctive features?"

"No... Nothing else," Angela answered, sounding drained.

"Okay," Maya said gently. "That's enough for now. You've been very helpful, Angela."

Maya's notebook was full of neatly written notes. Zack leaned back in his chair, letting out a breath he didn't realize he had been holding in.

His eyes drifted to the waitress who had served them, watching as she dealt comically with a customer who was attempting to loudly order something off-menu. A brief spark of laughter lit up Angela's tired eyes, and Zack felt a surge of relief. He knew the interrogation had been stressful on her.

He glanced over at Maya, noticing how she watched Angela with an empathetic, almost protective expression. He felt a rush of gratitude toward her. She had a knack for extracting information without causing further trauma—a rare attribute.

Just then, Zack's phone buzzed with a call from Riley.

"Tell me you've got something," he said.

"I've found your man," she said. "He's a North Korean operative, been living under the name Jeremiah Collins. He was in the Korean People's Army, and after coming to the States under a false identity, he lived in the same apartment building as our two missing employees this past summer."

"Sounds like he's the one we're looking for. Where does he live now?"

"Downtown D.C. But I think you'll find his job of greater interest than his address."

Zack waited, curious.

"He works in the D.C. Metro," Riley said. "Started there just last year."

"He's been scoping it out," Zack murmured, his voice full of conviction as he rose. "Because that's where the next attack is going to be."

* * *

The fluorescent lights of the Metro cast a pale glow on the commuters, who flowed like a current through the arteries of the underground. Zack kept his hand closed to his concealed pistol as he, Riley, and Maya wove through the throngs of people. The cavernous clatter of trains and chatter bounced off the tiled walls, but beneath it all was the silent hum of tension that only those in their line of work could sense.

"Keep your eyes peeled for anything out of place," Zack murmured into his earpiece, his voice a steady whisper amid the cacophony.

"Copy that," Riley said, her voice filling his ear. "How's your profiling going, Maya?"

"Thus far," Maya answered, "no luck. But I'll keep looking for anything suspicious."

"Riley, any luck with the cameras?" Zack asked, watching as a mother corralled her two children, her eyes never leaving them.

"Negative," she replied. "Whoever's behind this knows how to stay out of sight. I'm hacking into the maintenance schedules now to see if there's been any unauthorized access to service areas."

"Good. Keep at it," Zack said, his gaze sharp as he took in every face, every movement.

As he moved deeper into the station, Zack's focus honed in on the rhythm of the place—the ebb and flow of passengers, the predictable pauses as trains came and went. It was during one of these lulls that he spotted him—a figure detached from the pattern, a man whose gait was too deliberate, too measured.

"Guys, I've got something," Zack said softly, his pulse quickening. "There's a man, late thirties, wearing a janitorial uniform, but he doesn't seem...right."

"Where are you?" Riley's voice held an edge of urgency.

"Near the East corridor. I'm going to follow him." Zack slipped away from the main thoroughfare, his senses on high alert.

"Careful, Zack," Maya cautioned. "We don't have visuals on you anymore."

"Understood," he replied, stepping into the shadowed corridor.

The distance between them widened as Zack kept his target in view. The man glanced over his shoulder, an action that screamed 'guilty' to Zack's trained eye. He followed at a safe distance, blending into the environment by feigning interest in a Metro map displayed on the wall.

"Talk to me, Zack," Riley said.

"He's heading toward the utility area," Zack whispered, edging closer to the suspect who had now broken into a subtle but hurried pace. "Looks like he knows exactly where he's going—no hesitation."

"Stay on him," Riley said. "I'm working to get eyes on the area, but the security coverage is spotty at best."

"Roger that," Zack said, moving with purpose while keeping his demeanor casual.

Zack followed the suspect into a dim, narrow utility corridor. His footsteps echoed faintly in the tight space, the sound of distant trains a muted rumble through the concrete walls. He reached for his gun, the metal cool and reassuring against his palm.

"Entering the utility corridor," he said into the earpiece. "It's like a labyrinth down here—"

Before he could finish, shadows detached from the walls, coalescing into forms that were all too solid, all too threatening. Zack's reflexes, honed by years of training and fieldwork, kicked in. He ducked as a pipe swung where his head had been a split second before.

"Contact! Multiple assailants!" he shouted, rolling to the side to avoid a kick aimed at his ribs. He rose in one fluid motion, driving his fist into an attacker's solar plexus and following with an elbow strike to another's jaw.

"Zack, talk to us!" Riley's voice was tense with urgency.

"Busy at the moment!" Zack grunted, blocking a punch and countering with a swift punch of his own. The close quarters worked both for and against him; there wasn't much room to maneuver, but the same went for his attackers.

"Maya, with me!" Riley said. "We're on our way, Zack."

Their voices became distant in Zack's ears as he focused on the task at hand. Two men were down, but another lunged at him with a knife, the blade gleaming dully in the sparse light. Zack sidestepped, using the man's momentum to slam him into the wall.

"Where are you?" Maya's question cut through the chaos.

"North end of the utility corridor," he managed between breaths. "Near the—"

His words were cut off as another attacker blindsided him, tackling him to the ground. They grappled, Zack's fingers prying at the man's arm, which was wrapped around his throat in an attempt to choke him. With a surge of adrenaline, Zack flipped the assailant over and delivered a punishing blow.

"Almost there, Zack!" Riley barked.

The cavalry arrived just as Zack dispatched the last of his foes. Riley and Maya burst into the corridor, guns drawn and ready. Together, they swept the area, ensuring no more attackers lay in wait.

"Clear," Riley said, holstering her weapon as she surveyed the unconscious bodies.

"Good timing," Zack said, rubbing his neck where the attacker had tried to choke him. His heart still pounded, but the immediate danger had passed.

"Let's check them," Maya suggested, already kneeling beside the nearest body. "See if we can find any clues as to who they are or what they're doing here."

Zack did the same. His fingers worked efficiently, patting down pockets, searching for clues or intel.

"Nothing here," Riley reported, frustration edging her voice. "These guys are clean."

"Wait," Zack murmured, his hand closing around a slip of paper tucked inside a boot. He drew it out carefully, unfolding the crumpled edges to reveal rows of numbers and letters—a code that made little sense at first glance.

"Got something?" Maya asked, peering over his shoulder.

"Looks like a coded message," Zack said, his brain already shifting gears from combat to analysis. He recognized patterns and sequences, a skill that often felt like a sixth sense, whispering secrets meant to stay hidden.

"Can you make anything of it?" Riley asked, her gaze sharp and assessing.

"Not yet," Zack replied, scanning the code. Each character seemed random, but there had to be order amidst the chaos—a logic defined by the mind that had created it.

Zack's fingers danced over the crumpled note, his touch light as if the paper could dissolve under the pressure of his skin.

"Think, Zack," he muttered under his breath, his brow furrowed in concentration. The patterns evaded him, slippery and elusive like shadows cast by the flicker of candlelight. He could feel Riley's and Maya's eyes on him, their presence a silent encouragement, but the weight of responsibility bore down on him alone.

Then, all at once, it hit him. The code was a polyalphabetic cipher, complex but not impenetrable. He recalled a system his father had once shown him, a seemingly random assortment of letters that could unlock hidden messages when aligned correctly.

"Got it," he finally exclaimed, a triumphant edge to his voice. "It's a date and time—coordinates too." He rattled off the numbers, each digit slicing through the tension like a knife.

"Coordinates? To where?" Maya asked, leaning in closer.

"Here," Zack replied, pointing to a specific location on the Metro map plastered on the tunnel wall. "The central hub—the heart of the entire system."

"And the date?" Riley asked.

Zack set his jaw grimly. "Today. The date is today."

CHAPTER EIGHTEEN

The central hub of the D.C. Metro thrummed with the rhythm of the city's heartbeat, pulsing with the comings and goings of countless individuals. As Zack, Riley, and Maya stepped onto the wide concourse, Zack's eyes immediately canvassing the swarms of people, searching for anything out of place.

It was here, amidst the murmurs of hasty conversations and the clatter of hurried footsteps, that he suspected the next strike would occur. The encrypted note's warning had been as clear as it was cryptic:

They were on borrowed time.

"Riley, Maya, we need to move fast," he said. "Evacuate the area, but keep it subtle—we don't want to cause a panic." He could feel the weight of responsibility pressing down on him, a familiar burden that had only grown heavier since Montrose.

"Got it," Riley said, her tone equally composed. Her keen eyes began to sweep over the crowds, assessing each person as she moved through them, her NYPD training in full effect. Maya, ever the perceptive profiler, nodded in silent agreement.

As Riley and Maya hurried off, Zack's gaze darted from one passerby to another, analyzing their movements, their expressions—anything that might betray an ill intent. The air was dense with the electric charge of potential catastrophe. He traced the architectural lines of the station, noting exits, choke points, and structural vulnerabilities. Each step he took was measured, deliberate. His hand rested near his concealed sidearm, ready to draw at a moment's notice.

"See anything suspicious?" Zack asked, his voice crackling through the earpiece.

"Negative," Maya said. "People are complying, though. They think it's a drill."

"Keep it up. I'm heading deeper in," Zack said, pressing further into the belly of the hub. His senses were at their peak, finely tuned to detect the slightest hint of danger.

He moved through a swirling ocean of people, his eyes flicking between briefcases, bags, and the hands of those around him. The hum of the crowd filled the cavernous space beneath the city, a constant soundtrack to the urgency that gripped him.

As he neared the center of the concourse, his attention was pulled to a man huddled in a corner, his head bent over something obscured by a crumpled newspaper. Zack changed course immediately, threading his way through the crowd with single-minded focus. His heart pounded in rhythm with each footfall, but his face was as calm as a placid lake.

"Riley, Maya," he said, "I've got a possible suspect. Corner to the southeast, near the third vending machine."

"You need backup?" Riley asked.

"Not yet. You'll know if that changes."

Zack approached the man cautiously, his senses firing on all cylinders. The man's eyes darted up from behind the newspaper and locked onto Zack, looking puzzled.

"Can I help you?" the man asked.

Zack leaned closer and saw what the man had been concealing: a sandwich.

Zack sighed, relaxing. "No, I don't think you can. Sorry to disturb—"

He was cut off by a deafening roar that ripped through the concourse, followed by a shockwave that sent a shiver through the steel bones of the structure. Zack instinctively ducked down, his arms shielding his head as debris rained from above. A cloud of smoke and dust billowed outward, engulfing the area in an ashen shroud.

The man coughed, waving the newspaper in a futile attempt to dispel the dust.

"Riley? Maya?" Zack spat out the names, his throat raw from the sudden intake of dust.

"We're okay, Zack," Riley said, coughing. "We're unhurt."

"What about you?" Maya asked. There was an undisguised note of worry in her voice. "Are you injured?"

"No harm done," he said, wiping the back of his hand across his brow. The gritty film of dust and sweat clung to his skin, a testament to the close call they'd all just endured.

"Guess we figured out their plans," Riley said. "I'm surprised the blast wasn't bigger, though—they must've miscalculated the damage."

"Maybe," Zack murmured, but he wasn't convinced. The people they were dealing with were methodical, highly skilled operatives who didn't make rookie mistakes.

He took a moment, his chest heaving in the laborious effort to draw clean air into his lungs. "That blast...that can't be all they were planning. There must be something more."

"Zack," Riley warned, "you need to get out of there. Don't even think about—"

"Just make sure to get everyone out," he said, already jogging. "I need to figure out what's really going on."

The central hub loomed before him, its once orderly structure now marred by violence. The pungent smell of burning wires mingled with the acrid stench of explosives. Zack's pulse thrummed in his ears, a relentless reminder of what was at stake.

Pushing forward, Zack's thoughts whirled like the smoke around him. Was there another bomb? If so, where would they place it? Maximum impact—maximum casualties. It had to be somewhere crucial, somewhere devastating.

And then he saw it: a large, isolated maintenance panel, the ground beside it showing a series of overlapping prints.

His heart pounded in his chest, throbbing like a war drum. Every instinct screamed at him to run, to get as far away as possible. But he was not a man ruled by fear. He was a soldier, trained for these exact moments.

He approached the panel. Then, pulling out his pocket knife, he unwound the screws one by one, his eyes narrowing as he worked in a methodical yet hurried manner. The hum of his earpiece was a constant nagging in his ear, but he tuned out the worried calls from Maya and Riley, his focus locked onto the task at hand.

The last screw dropped to the ground with a soft clink. He hesitated for the briefest moment before pulling the panel off. The sight that awaited him made his blood run cold.

It was a nuclear bomb, its digital timer counting down with ruthless precision. And there were only a few minutes left.

"Guys," he said, trying to keep his voice steady, "I've found it. Nuclear. We're not just dealing with *a* bomb—we're dealing with *the* bomb."

"Holy shit, Zack..." Riley's voice trailed off, the gravity of the situation rendering her momentarily speechless.

"Evacuate everyone you can. Get the bomb squad on standby. I'll see what I can do from here."

"Are you insane? You're not trained for this!"

"Doesn't matter. There's no time." Zack's eyes locked onto the timer. The numbers seemed to drop faster than seconds should allow.

He approached the device, every step measured, every breath calculated.

His eyes narrowed as they scanned the malignant curves and wires of the bomb. Dust particles danced in the air, illuminated by the stark red countdown that cut through the haze like a beacon of impending doom. The device was a twisted sculpture of death, a patchwork of metal and circuitry that seemed to pulse with malevolence.

Then, he spotted a small handheld device connected to the bomb. It reminded him of the device used by the saboteurs at Montrose, the one Dr. Horowitz had helped build.

Was it possible Angela would know how to disable it?

"Riley," Zack said into his earpiece, "I need Angela Horowitz, now."

Seconds stretched into agonizing eons as he waited for the patch-through, his gaze locked onto the timer. Each flicker of the numbers downwards was a step closer to catastrophe.

"Dr. Horowitz is on the line," Riley said, her voice a mix of urgency and dread.

"Angela, it's Zack Force. I'm looking at what I believe is a second-generation version of the Montrose device. There's a digital timer, red wires leading to the main charge, and a secondary circuit board with a blue light flashing intermittently." He paused, trying to steady his breath.

"Okay, Zack, listen to me very carefully," Angela replied, her tone steely with concentration. "You can't afford any mistakes. A single misstep, and it could all be over."

Those words sliced through the fog of Zack's thoughts, sharpening his focus to a razor edge. His father had taught him composure under fire, the importance of a steady hand. Now, more than ever, those lessons mattered.

"I understand," he replied, his fingers hovering above the device as he awaited her instructions. "Guide me through this."

"First, you need to isolate the power supply to the timer. Look for a small panel on the side—there should be a series of wires inside."

Zack located the panel, his hands moving with deliberate care. The wires were a tangled web, a challenge laid out by someone who reveled in complexity.

"Next, you're going to disconnect the green wire, but only after you've grounded yourself on the frame of the device. Any static discharge could set it off."

He found the green wire, its color a sick mockery of something that should signify safety. Grounding himself, he gently pulled it free from its terminal. The timer continued its relentless countdown, indifferent to the sweat beading on Zack's brow.

"Good. Now, there's a fail-safe mechanism linked to the primary explosive. You'll see a silver box with a keypad on it," Angela continued, her voice steady in his ear.

Zack's eyes scanned for the silver box. His fingertips, slick with sweat, brushed against a cold metallic surface. There it was, nestled on the side of the wicked device. The keypad was a matrix of buttons, a series of numbers and symbols that could answer to only one correct combination.

"Got it," he said with a grunt.

"Now, this is the tricky part, Zack. You need to input the correct sequence, or else it'll trigger the detonation."

His heart pounded in his chest as he listened to her speak. Each word she spoke held the weight of destiny.

"I don't know," she said, sounding suddenly nervous."

"Come on, doc. Don't fail me now. What's your best guess?"

"It could be anything—a historical date, an anniversary, a birthday. Or maybe it's totally random."

Zack wiped sweat from his face. "I've gotta do something, doc."

Angela was silent for several interminable seconds. Then she snapped her fingers. "Wait a minute! One of the terrorists—he jokingly told me his name was Fibonacci."

"Okay..."

"So maybe this is a Fibonacci sequence. Input the numbers 1, 1, 2, 3, and 5."

Zack sucked in a sharp breath. The Fibonacci sequence meant that each number was the sum of the two preceding ones. His fingers hovered over the cold buttons, pressing each number with a precision born from desperation. As he inputted the last number, the blue light blinked out, replaced by a soft green glow.

"Did it work?" Angela's voice was strained, barely louder than a whisper.

"I think so," Zack replied, his hands trembling as he stepped back from the bomb. The timer had stopped ticking down, frozen at thirteen seconds. He let out a shaky breath he hadn't realized he'd been holding.

"You did well, Zack." There was relief in Angela's voice now, but it was also tinged with exhaustion. He could only imagine what kind of emotional rollercoaster she had been on, guiding him through the demon's labyrinth—and knowing that his life, and those of countless others, were in her hands.

Zack didn't immediately respond as he stared at the now inert bomb. His heart was still pounding, its rhythm echoing through his body like distant thunder. The remaining adrenaline in his veins made him feel shaky, but there was also an overwhelming sense of relief.

"Well," he said, his mouth dry, "now I think I'm going to get out of here. No sense sticking around in case—"

Before he could finish speaking, a wave of debris and dust struck him, throwing him back.

CHAPTER NINETEEN

The world had become a dizzying cacophony of screams and crumbling concrete. Dust hung like a shroud over the devastation, particles dancing in the scant rays of light that managed to penetrate the smoky haze.

Zack lay amidst the debris, consciousness grappling with the fog in his mind. The blast's echo still rang in his ears, now eerily silent without the familiar static of his earpiece—his lifeline to the outside now buried or blown to smithereens.

"Zack! Zack!" The voice seemed to claw its way through the thick air, desperate and distant. His name became a distorted chant, as if carried on the wings of the chaos that surrounded him. He tried to rise, to call out, but his body betrayed him, heavy as lead and twice as immobile. His lungs rejected the smoke-filled air, expelling it with violent coughs that shook his frame and clouded his vision with tears.

"Here!" he wanted to shout. "I'm here!" But the words were prisoners in his throat, muffled by the acrid taste of dust and fear.

Zack tried to piece together the fractured seconds before darkness had claimed him. The bomb...disarmed. But they had missed something: another explosive, hidden away like a viper in the grass. It had struck with precision, cruel and unforgiving.

The sharp sting of helplessness cut through him. He was supposed to be a warrior, not a casualty. Yet here he was, pinned beneath cold stone, unable to move, to protect, to serve. Anger rose within him, a fiery counter to the despair that threatened to engulf his spirit. He would not yield, not to terrorists, not to fate.

He tried to lift his head, but it felt tethered to the shattered concrete floor. His senses swam in the thick smoke that clawed at his throat, stealing the oxygen from his lungs.

"Zack!" It was Riley's voice, a beacon cutting through the haze of confusion and debris. "Hold on, we're almost there!"

Maya's silhouette emerged through the smoke, her eyes wide with concern. She crouched beside him, pressing her warm hand into his, her grip firm and reassuring. "You're going to be okay, Zack," she promised.

Riley knelt on the other side and began to clear the rubble from his pinned legs. The grating sound of shifting chunks of masonry filled the air, mingling with his labored breathing. Each movement sent shocks of pain radiating through him, but he welcomed it—it meant he was still alive.

"Stay with us, Zack," Riley said, glancing at him after removing a large piece of the wreckage. Her face was smeared with soot.

"Trying," he managed to say, but the effort to speak sapped his dwindling strength, and darkness edged his vision. He could feel himself slipping, consciousness ebbing away like the tide retreating from the shore.

"Zack!" Maya's voice was distant now, as if calling to him from another world. He wanted to respond, to reassure them, but the shadows reached up and pulled him down into their embrace.

In the void, time became irrelevant. Memories surged forward, shards of the past piercing the present. He was back in Afghanistan, the desert sun scorching his skin as he patrolled through a village with his unit. The weight of his gear was a familiar burden, and the rifle in his hands an extension of his will to protect.

"Force, cover the left flank," barked Sergeant Donovan, his voice crisp over the comms. Zack nodded, moving with practiced ease to secure their perimeter. They rounded a corner, and in an instant, chaos erupted. An IED detonated, and screams tore through the air.

"Man down! I repeat, man down!" The words were a guttural shout in his earpiece, but they seemed to come from far away as he watched his buddy, Jensen, fall to the ground, his leg torn open by shrapnel.

"Medic!" Zack yelled, dropping to his knees beside Jensen, applying pressure to the wound with trembling hands. Blood seeped through his fingers, hot and slick.

"Stay with me, man," he pleaded, locking eyes with the wounded soldier. Jensen's lips moved, mouthing a silent reply, but no sound reached Zack's ears.

"Force, we need you back here!" Sergeant Donovan's voice cut through the memory, pulling Zack back to the present—or was it still the past? He couldn't tell anymore. The lines between then and now blurred, pain and fear a common thread weaving through both times.

His father's face flashed before his eyes—strong, resolute, and kind. "Protect what you value the most," Douglas had said. Those words were a lifeline, a reminder of why he fought, why he endured.

"Zack," a voice called out to him, softer than before, yet insistent. Was it Riley? Maya? Or perhaps Sergeant Donovan? He couldn't discern. The call of duty was strong, but the darkness was stronger still, and once more, he surrendered to its call.

* * *

Consciousness crept back to Zack in fragments, like shards of glass slowly pieced together. The sterile scent of antiseptic wove through his senses before the muted beeps and hums of medical machinery followed suit. Slowly, his eyelids lifted, revealing a bleached-white ceiling that swam out of focus above him.

"Zack?" The voice was familiar, tinged with concern. It cut through the fog in his mind.

Turning his head slightly, he saw them—Riley and Maya, their faces looming over him like guardian angels cloaked in worry. Riley's brow was furrowed, her eyes scanning his face for signs of recognition. Maya's hand found its way to his arm, offering a silent strength.

"Hey," he managed, his voice no more than a raspy whisper. "How...how's everyone?"

"Everyone got out," Riley said with a relief so profound it almost seemed to physically lift from her shoulders. "We evacuated them just in time."

"Good," he croaked, pride swelling within his chest, pushing against the weight of his injuries.

Maya squeezed his arm gently. "You did it, Zack. The way you disarmed that bomb—you're a hero."

"Doesn't feel like it," he muttered, a wince crossing his features as he tried to shift his position. The pain was dulled, likely masked by whatever cocktail of drugs they had him on, but it was still there, a constant reminder of how close he'd come to not being here at all.

"Take it easy," Riley urged, placing a steadying hand on his shoulder. "You've been through a lot."

Zack wanted to argue, to tell them that resting was the last thing they should be doing when there were threats out there waiting to be neutralized. But his body betrayed him, demanding reprieve, and for once, he had no choice but to listen.

He lay back, still and silent, as feeling crept back into his body. Was he whole? He wiggled his fingers and toes, and they each responded. That was something.

The room's tranquility was broken by the sound of the door swinging open. A man in a white coat entered, a clipboard clutched in his hands. He approached Zack's bedside with a professional smile that didn't quite reach his eyes.

"Mr. Force, I'm Dr. Stein," he began, flipping through the papers on his clipboard.

"How bad is it, doc?" Zack asked.

"You've sustained a concussion, along with some minor lacerations and bruising. Remarkably, given the circumstances, nothing too serious or life-threatening. You're quite fortunate."

"That's one way to look at it," Zack replied with a dryness that belied his relief. "So I can leave?"

Dr. Stein's smile faltered. "I'd advise against it. You need rest, observation. A few days, at least."

"Days?" Zack echoed, frustration simmering behind his words. He attempted to sit up, but Riley's hand was firm on his shoulder, easing him back down.

"Listen to the doctor, partner," she said, her tone brooking no argument. "We can handle things for a while. You've earned some downtime."

"Riley's right," Maya said, her expression softening. "We'll take care of everything. You focus on getting better."

Zack's gaze shifted between the two women, seeing the genuine concern in their features. He knew they were capable, that they could manage without him temporarily, but it went against every fiber in his being to lie idle when there was a job to do.

"I'll come back in a little bit and check on you," Dr. Stein said. "For now, try to sleep as much as you can. Your body knows what to do."

With that, the doctor left the room.

Zack leaned back against the pillow. His head throbbed, each pulse a hammer against his temples. His eyes felt gritty as they took in the sterile white of the hospital room, the antiseptic smell mingling with a floral scent he assumed came from a get-well-soon bouquet somewhere out of sight. He shifted slightly, and pain lanced through him, reminding him of his brush with mortality in the metro.

"Riley," he croaked, voice barely above a whisper, "the explosions...any idea why there were two? In addition to the nuclear bomb, I mean?"

Riley frowned, her eyes holding that analytical glint Zack recognized from countless briefings. "We're thinking misdirection," she said, her words crisp and businesslike despite the concern shadowing her features. "First explosion could've been a primer to trigger evacuation routes into the path of the secondary – bigger – blast. Chaos breeds vulnerability."

"Or maybe," Zack mused aloud, trying to piece together the fragmented puzzle, "to draw first responders away from the real target." His mind spun, images of the chaos flashing like strobe lights behind his eyes.

"Could be," Riley agreed, nodding slowly. "And if that nuclear bomb had gone off..."

"Mass casualties," Zack finished for her, feeling the weight of what could have been. His fingers curled into the sheets, knuckles white. "Any leads on who planted them?"

"Zack," Maya chided gently, her tone softening. "You need to rest. Your body took a hell of a hit. We'll handle the investigation."

He wanted to protest, to demand every shred of intel, but he could see the logic in her eyes—and, more importantly, the firmness. Reluctantly, he sighed. "Just...keep me in the loop, okay?"

"Always," Riley promised, her hand resting on his arm for a moment—a gesture of solidarity.

The silence stretched between them, a palpable thing, as Zack closed his eyes and lay still. He heard Riley rise, her footsteps retreating until the faint click of the door signaled her exit. Maya remained, her presence an unspoken comfort. Then, with a quiet rustle of fabric, she too stood, lingering as if reluctant to leave him alone with his thoughts.

"Get some rest, Zack," Maya whispered, her voice tinged with something he couldn't quite name. The faint pressure of her hand squeezing his was both an anchor and a reminder of the fragility of life.

As the door closed behind her, Zack lay motionless, counting the seconds. Once assured of their departure, he peeled back the covers with wincing slowness. His body screamed in protest, but his will was ironclad; it propelled him upright, biting back groans of pain.

Careful not to jostle the IV line, he swung his legs over the side of the bed, muscles trembling with the effort. He planted his feet on the cold floor and stood, swaying like a reed in the wind. Gritting his teeth, he took one shaky step forward, then another, his determination a burning flame within his chest.

He glanced at the door, imagining the bustling hospital corridor beyond, filled with the living reminders of human vulnerability. He couldn't stay here, trapped in a bed, while threats loomed over the nation he had sworn to protect.

With painstaking care, Zack unhooked the IV, pressing a gauze pad to the site. He dressed in slow motion, movements deliberate, pulling on the clothes Riley and Maya had brought earlier. Each movement was agony, but the pain was a mere echo against the roar of duty calling him back to action.

Finally ready, he edged toward the door, pausing to brace himself against the wall. A deep breath steadied his resolve.

Then, with a last glance at the bed that had become his temporary cage, Zack stepped into the hallway and slipped into the anonymity of the hospital, disappearing like a ghost in pursuit of unfinished business.

CHAPTER TWENTY

"Home, sweet home," Zack murmured as he pushed open the door of the safe house.

It was a nondescript apartment nestled in the heart of old-town Alexandria, a place where history whispered through brick-lined streets and colonial lamp posts stood sentinel. The room's sparse furnishings – a worn leather couch, a coffee table scarred with rings from long-forgotten drinks, and a sturdy bookshelf – were illuminated by the creamy glow of a single floor lamp.

This would be his sanctuary, a place to lick his wounds away from prying eyes while he planned his next steps.

He sank into the couch, the leather creaking under his weight, and peeled back the bandage on his arm. The wound was angry, a vivid testament to the blast that had rocked the D.C. Metro, tearing metal and flesh alike. With mechanical precision, he cleaned and re-dressed it, the sting of antiseptic grounding him in the here and now.

His mind, however, was running ahead, threading through every possible outcome like a weaver at a loom.

"Where next?" he murmured to himself. He knew the terrorists' methods now—spreading both fear and destruction. They had struck a power plant, then the metro…

But where would they strike next?

The phone rang, shattering the silence. Zack glanced at the caller ID—Director Liz Murdock. He composed his features, schooling them into an expression of calm before answering.

"Zack," Liz said, "how are you holding up? They treating you well at the hospital?"

"Hey, Liz. Yeah, they're doing what they can." Zack's voice was even, betraying none of the throbbing pain that kept time with his heartbeat. "Docs are hovering, making sure I don't do anything foolish."

"Good. You need rest. Your body has been through a lot of trauma—don't underestimate that." There was steel in Liz's words, but underneath lay a river of concern.

"Rest is the plan," he lied smoothly, his gaze wandering around the room. "But you know me, always keeping one eye open."

"Zack..." Liz sighed, and he could almost see her hand pressed against her forehead in exasperation. "Just promise me you'll be careful. You're no good to us dead."

"Always careful, Liz," Zack replied, though they both knew it was only half-true. "Any updates on your end?"

"No breakthroughs, if that's what you mean," she said, and Zack could hear the rustle of papers, the background hum of the agency working tirelessly. "We're interrogating the suspects from the metro now, though. We'll get to the bottom of this."

The pain from Zack's injuries was a dull roar in the background of his mind, like distant artillery fire. He leaned back against the worn sofa, his body protesting with sharp stabs of complaint.

"Learned anything from them?" he asked.

There was a pause, as if the director was wondering if she should involve him.

"Come on, Liz," Zack said. "Humor a wounded, bedridden man."

She let out another sigh. "Well, the men who attacked you have been tight-lipped, but when they were being arrested, we overheard one of them say something about 'taking down the capital.' Probably just another reference to D.C., though."

"Maybe," Zack said, his thoughts churning.

"You think they meant something else?"

"I don't know," he replied noncommittally. He chuckled. "My brain's so addled right now, it's hard to even think straight."

"I'm sure it is." Liz was silent for a moment, and Zack sensed she was evaluating him, as if unsure if she could believe everything he was saying.

"Well," he said, "keep me in the loop if anything changes? I can only watch cable for so long."

"Of course," she said. "With any luck, though, I won't have to update you—you'll see it on the news."

"Of course," Zack agreed. Inwardly, though, he worried that if they didn't figure out the terrorists' plans soon, he might not like what the news had to report.

"Rest well, Zack."

"Thanks, Liz."

Zack ended the call and set the phone aside.

"Taking down the capital," he murmured to himself. D.C. was the obvious explanation...but what if they'd meant somewhere else? Somewhere like—

"Philadelphia," Zack whispered to the empty room. The city where American independence was declared, where the Founding Fathers had dreamed of a nation free from tyranny. The original capital. It made sense—too much sense.

He rose swiftly, ignoring the protestations of his battered body. Time was slipping through his fingers like grains of sand, and every second lost was a second closer to calamity. Philadelphia was the key, and he needed to be there to intercept whatever horror was planned.

He rose and hurried toward the door. There was no time to waste. The City of Brotherly Love was calling, and he had to answer—before it was too late.

* * *

The relentless thrum of the bullet train's engines filled Zack's ears as he settled into his seat, the fabric of which was a clinical shade of blue that did little to ease the tension in his muscles. His mind was a battlefield of strategy and anticipation, each thought another move against an unseen adversary. Philadelphia rushed closer with every mile the train devoured, carrying him toward an uncertain confrontation.

Zack was leaning back, contemplating sleep, when he noticed a figure across the aisle from him. The man was shrouded in a long, charcoal-colored trench coat, his face obscured by a low-brimmed hat. Something about him set Zack's teeth on edge—perhaps the way he seemed just slightly too aware of his surroundings.

Or maybe the barely visible bulge under his coat that suggested the presence of a concealed weapon.

There was something on the seat next to the man, a package wrapped in brown paper, and he kept touching it as if to reassure himself it was still there. The way his fingers brushed over the brown paper surface, almost affectionately, sent a pulse of suspicion down Zack's spine.

"Excuse me," Zack called to the attendant passing by, his voice measured despite the adrenaline beginning to percolate through his veins. "Could I get a coffee, black?"

"Of course, sir," the attendant replied with a practiced smile, moving on to fulfill the request.

Zack settled back in his seat, keeping an eye on the suspicious character from the corner of his eyes. The man must have sensed the weight of Zack's stare, because he shifted uncomfortably before standing, the package clutched close to his side. With a casual glance around, the man started making his way toward the front of the car, threading through the human tapestry with careful steps.

Zack's mind churned with possibilities. A Trojan horse entering Philadelphia? Could this anonymous traveler be the harbinger of chaos, or was paranoia painting every shadow as a threat?

"Here's your coffee, sir." The attendant's voice broke through his musings, offering a steaming cup.

"Thank you," Zack murmured, barely registering the warmth seeping into his palms. He took a sip, allowing the bitter liquid to ground him briefly as he watched the suspect disappear into the next compartment.

It would be reckless to confront the man without evidence, yet intuition gnawed at Zack—a primal instinct that had saved his life more times than he could count. His father had taught him to trust that feeling, and he couldn't afford to ignore it now.

Taking a deep breath to steady his nerves and quell the pain that still lingered from the metro blast, Zack rose. His movements were deliberate, a predator stalking his prey, mindful of the delicate dance between hunter and hunted.

"Sir, you should remain seated while the train is in motion," the attendant cautioned, eyeing him with mild concern.

"I just need to stretch my legs," Zack replied with a reassuring nod, trying not to betray the urgency that propelled him forward. "I won't go far."

As the attendant moved on, Zack slipped into the stream of passengers, his gaze fixed on the stranger now threading through the crowded compartments ahead. Zack's jaw clenched, each step forward a measure of resolve against the persistent throb in his skull.

"Excuse me," he muttered repeatedly, his voice barely more than a rasp as he maneuvered past chattering tourists and weary businesspeople. He was a ghost haunting the narrow aisles, driven by instinct and the solemn oath he'd taken to defend against unseen threats.

Can't lose him, Zack thought, the image of the suspicious package burning in his mind like a brand.

"Ticket, sir?" a voice called out, momentarily pulling him from his pursuit.

"Later," he grunted without breaking stride, his gaze locked onto the retreating form of the suspect. The attendant frowned but said no more, his attention drawn away by another passenger's inquiry.

As Zack passed the galley, gaining ground on his quarry. The claustrophobia of the space seemed to amplify every heartbeat, every breath.

He was close enough now to note the tension in the man's shoulders, the way his fingers clutched the package with a possessive urgency. Zack's own hand hovered near the concealed holster under his jacket, a silent promise of action if needed.

The corridor narrowed as they approached the end of the car, and for a moment, Zack felt the walls press in on him, a tangible echo of the pressure mounting within his chest.

A heavyset woman climbed out of a seat to the left, blocking Zack's path as she bent and swept cracker crumbs off her seat. "Excuse me, ma'am," Zack said with forced politeness, but there was no way around her.

She gave him a withering look. "That's what's wrong with this country," she muttered. "Nobody shows any manners any more."

She shook her head at him, as if to drive home her disappointment in him, before retaking her seat. Zack hurried past her, searching for the man he'd been following.

The man, however, had disappeared.

Zack cursed inwardly. Where had the man gone?

Just as Zack was slipping past the bathroom, the door flew open, striking his arm and pushing him back. The man lunged at him with a knife.

The sliver of light caught on the blade's edge was the only warning Zack received before the man threw his entire weight behind a swift, deliberate strike. Adrenaline fueled his reflexes as he parried the attack with the injured arm, wincing as the cold steel bit into his jacket sleeve.

"Should've stayed in your seat," the man sneered, his voice as cold and hard as the weapon he brandished. He lunged again, this time aiming low, but Zack was ready.

Using his uninjured arm, he delivered a powerful punch to the man's stomach. The attacker stumbled backward, unprepared for Zack's quick retaliation. Ignoring the pulsating pain that threatened to consume him, Zack pulled his own weapon from its holster, training it on the crumpled form of his assailant.

"Don't move," he said. He kicked the knife away from the man's reach and quickly retrieved a pair of handcuffs from his pocket. He snapped one cuff around the man's wrist and then secured him to an overhead rail.

Ignoring the startled gasps and horrified whispers of the passengers who had witnessed the altercation, Zack turned his attention to the abandoned package still lying on the bathroom floor. It was a nondescript brown parcel tied with string, like something out of an old spy novel.

"What's in it?" Zack asked.

The man smirked. "Wouldn't you like to know?"

Zack debated waiting for a bomb squad. If he opened the package, he might set it off. If he waited, though, the bomb might go off anyway.

Damned if I do, damned if I don't.

He chose the proactive path. With deliberate care, he began to untie the knot, ensuring not to jostle it too much—the memory of the explosion in the metro was still ringing in his ears.

"Tick-tock," muttered the subdued man. "Better be careful you don't trigger it."

"Shut up," Zack growled, focusing on the task at hand. The last loop gave way, and he unfolded the paper. Inside, he found a box filled with…

Nothing but shredded newspaper and a mocking smiley face drawn on a slip of card. A decoy. His heart sank, yet the ember of rage kindled deep within him.

"Where is it?" Zack demanded, whipping his head toward the man. His voice was a blade, sharp and cold. "Where is the real target?"

The man's laughter grated against Zack's resolve. "Oh, you really are quite entertaining. It's already too late to stop it."

"Tell me!" Zack shouted, his hand gripping the man's collar, pulling him close enough to feel each other's breaths.

The man laughed in his face. "You'll find out soon enough. I'm sure it'll be all over the news."

Inside Zack's mind, the gears turned frantically. If Philadelphia was a ruse, then where? His thoughts spiraled, seeking connections in the spiderweb of information he possessed.

Zack's pulse hammered in his temples, every beat a reminder of the stakes. For a fleeting moment, the image of his father flashed before him: stern, unyielding, a soldier to the end. It steeled his resolve. This country, its people—they were what he valued, what he had sworn to defend.

"Your little game ends here," Zack said, shoving the man back against the wall. Passengers recoiled, their eyes wide with shock.

The man chuckled darkly. "No, my friend. The game is just beginning, and you can't even see the board."

CHAPTER TWENTY ONE

The chill of the descending night settled on Zack's skin as he stepped off the train onto the platform in Washington, D.C. The fluorescent lights of Union Station flickered overhead, casting sharp shadows that danced around him like specters from his recent brush with death.

He adjusted his jacket, feeling the stiffness of his healing wounds beneath the fabric, a constant reminder of the blast that had nearly claimed his life.

"Zack!" Director Liz Murdock's voice cut through the hum of the station like a bullet, her tone laced with a mix of concern and reprimand. Her piercing eyes locked onto his.

"Damn it, Zack, what were you thinking?" she demanded, approaching him with brisk steps, her tailored suit immaculate despite the late hour. "Sneaking out of the hospital? Lying to me?"

"Liz," Zack began, his voice steady despite the underlying ache that thrummed through his body. "I'm fine. We don't have time for me to be lying in a bed when—"

"Fine?" Riley interjected, arms crossed over her chest, her brow furrowed with worry that contradicted the steel in her voice. "You were unconscious when we found you buried in rubble in the metro, Zack. You should still be at the hospital."

"Reckless or not, I'm here now," Zack said, meeting Riley's gaze.

Before the argument could escalate further, Maya Walsh stepped forward. "Look, I get it," she said, her voice a calm anchor amidst the rising storm of emotions. "You just wanted to help."

He nodded. "That's right."

Liz started to cut in, but Maya kept going. "And the most important thing right now," she said, "is to figure out where they're attacking next and to stop them. We're all agreed on that, aren't we?"

Liz sighed, her gaze softening as she glanced from Maya to Zack. "She's right," she admitted, her tone lacking its usual bite. "But you're in no state to be in the field, Zack. You could barely stand up when you got off the train."

Zack bristled at Liz's words. He was still sore and weak from the explosion, dull ache lingered in his side where a piece of shrapnel had sliced through his flesh, but that didn't mean he couldn't do his job.

"I'm still capable," he said. "Besides, you need me."

Liz stared back, as if preparing a counter response. But this time, it was Riley who interrupted.

"We need to focus on where they're striking next," she said. "If Philadelphia was a smokescreen, what's the real target?"

The question hung heavy in the air, pulling at Zack's attention like a magnet. He thought of that phrase the terrorists had used: 'taking down the capital.'

"Could be anything," he muttered, rubbing his temple where a dull throb had taken residence. "Historical landmarks, government buildings, public gatherings...they want maximum impact."

"Transport hubs?" Riley suggested.

"Too obvious." Zack shook his head. "After the Metro incident, security there is tighter than ever."

"Then what about symbolic targets?" Maya asked. "Places that represent American power, freedom, democracy..."

"Capital," he murmured, the word echoing in his mind like a haunting refrain from an old, forgotten song.

"Zack?" Riley asked. "You're zoning out on us."

But Zack's gaze was distant, his focus narrowing as if peering through a sniper's scope. The pieces fell into place, each click resounding in his head with the weight of revelation.

"Capitol," he corrected himself, his tone sharpening. "With an *o*, not an *a*. What if they meant the Capitol Building?"

Liz's eyebrows knitted together in a frown. "You think they've been playing a game of semantics with us?"

"Exactly," Zack affirmed. "Think about it—the Capitol Building, the very symbol of our nation's legislative power. Its destruction would be more than just an attack—it'd be a statement."

He looked up, picturing the grand dome of the Capitol, imagining the chaos that would ensue should it come under attack. The thought chilled him to the bone.

"Wait," Riley interjected, her hand going to her pocket. She pulled out her phone, thumbing through messages with a speed born of necessity. Her breath caught, and she held up the screen for the others to see—a notification from their intelligence network.

"An anonymous tip came in," she explained, her words clipped with tension. "A large purchase of ammonium nitrate fertilizer – enough to make a substantial bomb – was made recently. It wasn't flagged because it was bought in small batches across multiple states."

Director Liz exhaled sharply, her face etching into a map of concern and command as she processed this new information. "That could just be a farmer preparing for planting season," she reasoned, but Zack saw the doubt in her eyes.

"Or it could be them stockpiling for another attack," Maya countered. "Combine that with the chatter we've intercepted about 'making a statement' and 'a show of force'..."

"Can we afford to take that chance?" Riley asked, her gaze locked with Liz's, imploring her to understand the magnitude of the risk.

"Damn it," Liz muttered, finally conceding. "I'll contact Capitol security, see if anything's amiss."

Zack watched the director step away to make her call. He felt Riley's gaze on him.

"How sure are you about this, Zack?" Riley asked.

"Pretty darn," he said. "It fits." *And I hope I'm right,* he thought, *because if not, then we're completely in the dark.*

A moment later, Liz returned, looking pale.

"What did they say?" Riley asked.

"That's just it—I couldn't reach anyone there. Nobody is answering their phones."

* * *

The night air was thick with uncertainty as Zack settled into the cramped interior of the mobile surveillance unit parked in the shadows near the Capitol Building. The monitors cast a ghostly glow on the faces of Riley and Maya, who were scanning the feeds with hawk-like intensity. Zack's gaze was fixed on the screen that displayed the iconic dome, a sentinel in the silence of the night.

"Anything yet?" he asked.

"Awfully quiet," Riley said.

A truck rumbled past on a nearby street. Zack could feel the pulse of the city around them, unaware of the dangers that lurked in the darkness.

"How's the evacuation going?" Zack asked.

"We've managed to evacuate most of the surrounding homes," Maya said. "As far as the staff inside, if we try evacuating them now, we'll just tip our hand. It's also possible they've already been tied up or otherwise removed from the equation, like the security."

Zack hoped the terrorists had only restrained the security rather than killing them. He wouldn't know for sure, however, until he entered the building.

"Then I'll head in with my team," he said, "so we'll be able to respond if anything happens."

Both women gazed at him, their eyes solemn. He nodded at them.

"Good luck, both of you," he said, allowing a rare, genuine smile to surface, a momentary crack in his otherwise impenetrable facade. It was a soldier's acknowledgment, an understanding that they each carried a piece of the other's life in their hands.

"Back at you," Riley said.

"Stay safe," Maya added.

With a final glance at the screens, Zack rose from his seat, feeling the familiar surge of adrenaline flood his system. His body protested with flashes of pain, but he pushed through it, driven by a purpose that transcended physical limitations. He was more than just a man; he was a symbol of the fight against the insidious shadow of terror that loomed over his country.

Stepping out of the surveillance unit, Zack took a deep breath of the chilled air, letting it fill his lungs and steel his resolve. The night may have been quiet for now, but he knew the silence was a deceiver, and beneath it lay the potential for chaos that he was determined to thwart. He glanced toward the Capitol Building, its silhouette majestic against the dark sky, and felt the weight of history upon him.

The tactical unit was waiting for him just a few paces away, a tapestry of shadows against the moonlit rectangle of tarmac. Their gear reflected the battle-hardened resolve in their eyes, a mirror to Zack's own.

"Alright, listen up," Zack said, his voice steady as he faced his team. They were a mixture of seasoned agents and elite soldiers, each one handpicked for their skill and nerve. They stood before him, ready and expectant, their own resolve reflected in the sharp lines of their camouflaged faces.

"Tonight, we're not just defending a building; we're defending the heart of our nation. The enemy believes they can strike at the core of our democracy, sow chaos and fear," he continued, his gaze sweeping over the faces of his comrades. "But they've forgotten who they're dealing with. We are the guardians standing between order and anarchy, and we will not falter."

He paused, allowing his words to sink in, to kindle the fire he knew burned within each of them. "Remember your training, watch each other's backs, and stay sharp. We're the line that holds tonight. For every citizen asleep in their beds, for every child that dreams of a better tomorrow—we hold the line."

"Sir, we won't let you down," a voice said.

"Good. Let's move out," Zack said, turning on his heel. With a symphony of boots on pavement, they advanced toward the Capitol, a silent phalanx in the darkness.

The grandeur of the Capitol Building loomed before them, its iconic dome a sentinel against the night sky. Under normal circumstances, it would have been a sight to instill pride and patriotism. Tonight, however, it was a battleground waiting to be defended, a symbol under threat.

As they approached, Zack's eyes automatically scanned the perimeter. The stillness was unsettling, the absence of movement unnatural. Something was off.

"Riley, do you have eyes on the guards?" Zack whispered into his comms, keeping his voice low.

"Negative, Zack. I'm not seeing any activity on my end, either."

"Something's not right here," Zack murmured, his instincts now buzzing with alarm.

His team spread out, moving in practiced formation, each member hyper-aware of their surroundings. Zack's eyes darted from shadow to shadow, searching for any sign of the missing guards. The emptiness where there should have been the routine presence of security personnel screamed danger.

"Echo-1, we are approaching the east wing entrance," Zack whispered into his comm, his voice barely more than a breath against the stillness of the night.

"Copy, Echo-1," Maya replied. "No movement on thermal scans. Proceed with caution."

His fingers brushed against the cold, unyielding solidity of his weapon, a comforting familiarity in this rapidly escalating situation. His heart pounded a rhythmic tattoo against his ribcage, each throb echoing the tension that was slowly unfurling within him and his team. They were walking into the unknown, into a situation fraught with uncertainty and peril. Yet, they pressed on, driven by duty and the promise they'd made to uphold order.

Silently, they reached the massive double doors that marked the entrance to the east wing. Zack signaled for Peters, their tech expert, to approach. Peters moved with the quiet precision of a panther, his gloved hands deftly maneuvering a small device from his utility pouch. With a few expert tweaks, he attached it to the lock mechanism.

"Stand by," Peters whispered, his fingers dancing over the controls on the device. There was an all-encompassing silence as they waited, their collective breaths seemingly suspended in time.

A soft click cut through the silence, and a slight push was enough to open the immense doors. They swung slowly, revealing a wide hallway. The usually bustling corridor was eerily deserted, the only sound being the low hum of the fluorescent lights overhead. The silence was deafening, an absence of noise that fell heavily and thickly onto Zack's ears like wet wool.

"Clear," Peters murmured, moving stealthily into the corridor, his night vision goggles scanning for any sign of life. But there was nothing—no guards, no technicians, not even the janitorial staff they expected to see at this hour. It was as if the beating pulse of the building had simply stopped.

Zack's senses screamed danger, but still, they had a mission to complete. With a nod, he motioned his team forward through the yawning entrance. The silence took on an almost physical aspect, wrapping around them like a shroud as they infiltrated deeper into the heart of democracy.

"Overwatch, give me updates every five," Zack commanded into his comms, trying to keep his growing unease from seeping into his voice.

"Copy that," Maya's voice crackled in response, a thin thread of reassurance in this echoing void.

"Prepare for room-to-room," Zack instructed his team in a low murmur. The chilling silence dictated the need for meticulous caution; their communication had to be minimal, their movements precise. Each one of them understood the inherent risk of what they were about to undertake.

In response to his command, the team moved as one. Their steps were methodical, calculated, the vibrations whispering through the cold marble underfoot. The Capitol's grand halls seemed to hold their breath in anticipation, the ornate murals and golden insignia a haunting backdrop to their intrusion. Each closed door was a potential ambush, each corner a tactical obstacle.

Stepping lightly, Zack led the team down the corridor, his heart pounding like a war drum in his ears. The eeriness of this place was different from their usual battlefield. Here, they weren't just soldiers;

they were protectors of an ideal that had suddenly become fragile and vulnerable.

Zack's team started opening doors and clearing rooms. Spotting a door on his left, Zack eased it open and stepped inside.

A few dozen people – staff and security – sat on the floor, their hands and feet bound with zip ties, their mouths gagged, their eyes pleading for help.

"Get these people out of here," Zack whispered to the man next to him, who drew a knife and began cutting ties.

Zack returned to the hall and continued to advance. Then, just as he was about to breach the door leading to the senate chamber, Maya's urgent voice filled his ear.

"I've got multiple thermal signatures rapidly closing in on your position. They're coming from the direction of—"

That was as much as Zack heard before an assault rifle shattered the stillness of the building.

CHAPTER TWENTY TWO

Minho Choi's fingers danced over the tablet that connected him to an array of security cameras, his gaze locked onto the grainy footage being fed back from another part of the Capitol Building. The screen showed a team of American operatives moving through the corridors, their tactical gear barely visible against the shadows.

Suddenly, the corners of Minho's lips curled upwards into a smirk as figures emerged from the darkness, the silent ambush unfolding like a well-rehearsed play.

"Exactly as predicted," Minho uttered to the humming machines around him, the only witnesses to his imminent triumph. His heart raced not from fear but exhilaration. They had wandered into his trap like lambs.

Minho's operators closed in, their weapons raised with lethal intent. The dance of death played out on the screens, and Minho watched with rapt attention, savoring every detail.

"Is trapping rats always this satisfying?" he mused aloud, though the question was rhetorical. He already knew the answer, felt the rush of power surge through him as the Americans were ensnared within his web.

As the confrontation intensified on screen, Minho leaned back into the plush leather chair that served as his command throne, allowing himself a rare moment of reflection. This wasn't just another operation; it was the fulfillment of a destiny decades in the making.

"Father," he whispered, the word a sacred mantra, "we are moments away from delivering the message." His father, who had instilled in him the flames of vengeance and the burden of purpose, was the silent shadow that had guided him to this very room.

"America will feel the sting of humility today," Minho continued, his thoughts spinning with fervor. "To bring a giant to its knees...there is no greater statement for our country, for our people." The bomb, hidden within the very heart of democracy, would be his magnum opus, his gift to a world he believed needed to be shaken from its complacency.

"Today, I am the hand of justice," he declared, his voice steady, his conviction unshakable. "The rotten tree that is this corrupt nation will fall, and from its ashes, new growth will emerge."

His eyes, dark orbs reflecting the chaos he was about to unleash, never left the screen as he watched the American operatives struggle against his men. They fought valiantly, he'd give them that, but it was all in vain. The stage was set, the actors in place, and the final act was about to begin.

Then, slowly, Minho Choi's smirk faltered, the lines of his face hardening as he witnessed one of the operatives, against all odds, begin to dismantle the trap set for him. On the grainy camera feed, a spectacle unfolded that Minho had not anticipated. The soldier – his name was Zack Force, and he had been a thorn in Minho's side every step of the way – moved with a lethal grace, parrying blows and disarming assailants with a precision that betrayed years of training and an unyielding will to survive.

"Impossible," Minho muttered under his breath, the room around him fading into nothingness as he fixated on the screen. The other operatives were well-trained, ruthless even, but here was Zack—outnumbered, outgunned, but not outmatched.

The air was tense, electric with unspoken curses, as each fallen operative only seemed to bolster Zack's momentum. Minho's fingers twitched, itching to intervene, but he remained rooted, watching the drama unfold. He couldn't afford to look away, not when so much was at stake.

"Keep moving," he willed silently, eyes trained on Zack's relentless advance through the hallowed halls. Minho's pulse quickened, not with fear, but with the thrill of the chase. The Capitol Building, with its labyrinthine corridors and grandiose rooms, now served as a stage for their deadly dance.

"Your bravery is commendable, Zack Force," Minho spoke to the empty room, his voice cool and detached. "But it changes nothing."

Minho watched, his chin resting in his palm, as the Americans edged nearer to the bomb's location.

"Such a shame, really," Minho mused, his thoughts weaving through scenarios and contingencies. "To destroy such talent. But it is necessary. For the greater good."

Minho decided he had waited long enough. His fingers danced across the console, arming the device that would be his opus. The screen before him split between the camera feed and the bomb's activation sequence—a digital countdown ticking away with grim inevitability.

"Engage them now," Minho said into his ear piece, his voice a low rumble of thunder. "And make it spectacular."

His agents sprang into action like hounds released from their chains, the cacophony of gunfire erupting within the hallowed halls. Zack Force, the tenacious American agent, was cornered but fought like a wild beast pushed to the edge of its territory.

With the melee providing the perfect diversion, Minho rose from his chair, the fabric of darkness enshrouding him as he slipped out into the corridor. He moved with the grace of a wraith, threading his way through the building.

Agent Force may have courage, he thought, *but bravery is no match for destiny.*

Minho's heart thrummed with the thrill of the hunt and the pride of the hunter. This was more than retribution; this was the rewriting of history, the pen poised to strike through centuries of lies and deception.

"Like a surgeon excising a tumor," he mused. "A necessary cut to heal the body."

The corridors whispered secrets of power and conspiracy as Minho navigated them, every shadow a potential ally, each flicker of light a deceptive foe.

"Impossible," he assured himself, the mantra a shield against doubt. "They will not disarm it. They cannot."

For Minho had conjured a puzzle wrapped in enigma, shielded by riddles. His bomb was not merely a device of destruction—it was an impenetrable fortress of complexity, designed to withstand the most cunning of assaults. He had studied, learned, and improved from the last time, creating something far superior, unassailable.

"Let them try," he whispered as he surged forward. "Let them throw themselves against the walls of my creation."

In his mind's eye, he saw the intricate wiring, the layers of safeguards, each one a testament to his genius. It was, he knew, his masterpiece, the culmination of his life's work—and his contribution to the world stage.

His hand brushed against the cold marble wall, feeling the pulse of the nation it housed. A surge of exhilaration coursed through him. He was moments away from triumph, the herald of a new dawn.

History will remember me, Minho declared within the confines of his thoughts. *Not as a villain, but as the harbinger of true change.*

Just then, he heard the rapid approach of footsteps. He pressed himself into an alcove's shadowy embrace, gun drawn, breath held in silent anticipation. The footsteps grew louder, boots striking marble with the authority of a man on a mission.

Move, he mentally urged the unseen interloper, willing the echo to fade into nothingness. His fingers tightened around the gun's grip, its cold metal a sharp contrast to the warmth seeping from his palm.

Finally, silence reclaimed its dominion over the hallway. Minho counted three heartbeats, then three more, before daring to emerge from his temporary sanctuary. He moved with the fluid grace of a specter, his steps light, almost ethereal against the stone floor.

But as he rounded a corner, the shadows coalesced into solid form, and Zack Force stepped out, a gun aimed squarely at Minho's chest.

"Where is it?" Zack demanded, his voice a razor-edged whisper that cut through the silence.

Minho met his gaze, an inscrutable mask concealing the maelstrom within. "Where is what, Agent Force?" he replied, his tone dripping with feigned innocence.

Zack showed no surprise at the mention of his name. "The bomb. Where's the bomb?"

"Ah, that," Minho said, tilting his head ever so slightly. "I'm afraid that information is not for the likes of you."

"Cut the crap," Zack snapped. "People will die."

"Die?" Minho echoed, his lips curling into a bitter smile. "It is often said, 'To make an omelet, one must break a few eggs.' America is corrupt, Agent Force—a bloated carcass, ripe with decadence and greed. It needs to be brought down like a rotten tree to make room for new growth."

"Is that so?" Zack's face hardened. "And you think you're the lumberjack?"

"History is replete with men who have felled empires," Minho retorted. "I am merely a humble gardener, pruning away disease to let the healthy plants thrive."

"Pruning with explosives isn't gardening, it's madness," Zack countered, his finger steady on the trigger. "You can end this now. Where's the bomb?"

"Madness?" Minho laughed, though there was no humor in it. "No, Agent Force. This is but the inevitable consequence of your country's arrogance. You see, the roots of a great nation run deep, yet they are not immune to rot. And when the foundation is infested, the tree must fall. That is the natural order of things."

"Natural order or not, I can't let you do this." Zack's eyes narrowed, his resolve clear.

"Of course you can't," Minho acknowledged with a nod, his mind spinning with each possible outcome. "But ask yourself, Agent Force, are you truly capable of stopping the inevitable?"

They stared at one another, neither backing down. If they stayed here much longer, it wouldn't matter what either of them wanted—the bomb would decide for them.

"Put the gun down," Zack said.

Minho's fingers curled tighter around his pistol, the contours so familiar they might have been an extension of his own flesh. His gaze locked onto Zack's – a mirror of conviction – and in that instant, Minho saw the embodiment of everything he sought to obliterate.

"Your cause is over," Zack continued, his tone steady, though the faint lines of strain around his eyes betrayed the weight of the day. "This ends now. Put your weapon down and tell me where the bomb is."

Minho's lips twisted into a wry smile. Here stood a man who believed in salvation, in saving the world from the very fires Minho yearned to unleash. It would be admirable if it weren't so tragically misguided.

"Agent Force," Minho began, his voice calm despite the adrenaline that thrummed through his veins. "You stand for a nation that spreads its roots like a plague. My life, my death—they are but water and sunlight to the new seeds that will sprout from the ashes of your decay."

His finger flinched toward the trigger. To die here, now, would be to seal his commitment, to etch his beliefs into history with the finality of blood. This was his stage, his performance.

His sacrifice.

"Damn it!" Zack's voice was edged with frustration, the agent's facade cracking to reveal the human beneath. "Don't make me do this Where is the bomb?"

But Minho knew better than to betray his masterpiece; his magnum opus would sing its destructive aria without interruption. He took a slow, deliberate breath, savoring the taste of power, of destiny.

"Corruption must be purged," he whispered, almost to himself, as if reciting a prayer to the gods of chaos he served. And then, with the serenity of a martyr embracing the pyre, Minho Choi raised his weapon.

CHAPTER TWENTY THREE

The air hung heavy with the acrid scent of gunpowder, mixed with a metallic tang that Zack knew all too well—blood. A man lay sprawled on the ornate carpet of the Capitol Building, its intricate patterns marred by the darkening pool spreading from beneath him.

"Damn shame," he muttered.

Zack crouched beside the body, his fingers searching for a pulse at Minho's neck, where the skin was still warm. The pulse was there, but faint. That was good—he had a lot to answer for.

"Zack, do you copy?" Riley's voice crackled through the earpiece, a lifeline to sanity in the midst of chaos.

"Copy," he said. "I think I just shot the man responsible for all this nonsense. I need a medic in here."

"I'll send someone right away. Did he say anything before you shot him?"

Zack's mind replayed the final moments in his mind. "I think there's a bomb," he murmured, scanning the grand corridor for any clue that might have been left behind. "We need to find it."

"Understood. We're on it." The line went silent as Riley and Maya presumably turned their attention to the feeds from the surveillance cameras.

A pair of security guards emerged then. "I need you to take charge of this prisoner," he told them. "Watch him closely, and see to it that he gets medical attention."

Hurrying past the two guards, Zack jogged down the hallway, trying to think of the most logical place for planting a bomb in this building. His hands were slick on the grip of his weapon, senses on high alert for the telltale ticking or the subtle whiff of explosives.

"Riley, Maya, you see anything suspicious on the cameras?" he asked, his eyes scrutinizing every shadow, every alcove.

"Nothing yet," Maya replied, her tone taut with concentration. "The building's a labyrinth, Zack. It could be hidden anywhere."

"Keep looking," he urged, his gut clenching at the thought of what a bomb could do to this historic edifice—the heart of American democracy. And more importantly, what such an attack symbolized.

A sudden realization struck him, a piece of the puzzle clicking into place. The man he'd killed had been cunning, methodical. He would've hidden the bomb in a location unlikely to be disturbed, somewhere remote.

Each corner he turned, every shadowy crevice he scanned, felt like a race against an unseen clock. His mind, a whirring processor of possible locations for the bomb, discarded each area that lacked strategic value.

Then, as if guided by some divine sense of duty, his focus narrowed on a door at the far end of the corridor—solid oak, reinforced.

"Riley," Zack said, his voice terse as he approached the door, "I found something. A locked door, looks heavy-duty."

"Got it, I'm pulling up the blueprints now. That section is supposed to be open storage..." Riley replied, her words dissolving into the hum of keystrokes.

"Stand by," Zack said, sizing up the door. He tried the door, but it was locked. No surprise there. He took a step back, assessing its strength, the position of the hinges.

"Here goes nothing," he murmured, charging at the door. The solid oak buckled under his weight, but held firm. Zack grunted, feeling the impact reverberate through his skeleton. He backed off again, rolling his shoulder to shake off the dull pain. He glanced around, his eyes landing on a fire extinguisher encased in glass.

With a swift elbow jab, he shattered the glass, earning himself a handful of tiny cuts flecked with blood. Ignoring the stinging sensation, he yanked out the hefty cylinder and took another look at the door.

He swung the extinguisher into the door near where he guessed the lock would be. The impact sent a shockwave up his arm and echoed down the corridor. Again and again, he beat the door until the metal groaned and finally gave way. He stepped in.

The room lay in darkness, save for the ominous glow of a digital countdown. There it was, nestled among boxes of discarded files and construction tools—the bomb. Its design was sleek, menacing in its simplicity; the counter was a glaring red, ticking down with relentless certainty.

The room felt like a vacuum, every sound sucked away except for the ticking of the bomb. Zack's ears thrummed with the intensity of his heartbeat as he crouched beside the device that could reduce the Capitol to rubble. He keyed his comm device, a lifeline to the outside world.

"Maya, Riley," Zack's voice was calm but carried an edge of urgency, "I've got eyes on the bomb. It's armed and counting down."

"Dr. Horowitz is ready," came Riley's reply, her words clipped with tension. "Patching her through."

"Zack?" Angela's voice crackled through the speaker. "Describe the device to me."

He scanned the bomb: a mess of wires, a circuit board heart, a digital countdown marching toward zero. "It's housed in a metal casing—about two feet by one foot. There's a keypad, a digital screen, and more wires than a server farm. The timer's set for..." Zack paused, squinting at the red digits. "...under fifteen minutes now."

"Look for a serial or model number," Angela said.

"Nothing," Zack said after a moment, frustration gnawing at him.

"Okay," Angela said slowly. "Then see if you can find the power source."

His hands moved over the device, steady despite the drumroll of his pulse. He found the battery compartment.

"Got it. Now what?"

"Disconnect it carefully," she said.

Sweat trickled down his brow, each tick of the countdown like a hammer on an anvil. His hands trembled slightly as he reached for the power source, reminding himself to remain steady. His fingers moved delicately over the bomb's cruel anatomy like a surgeon operating on a patient.

"Okay...I've disconnected the power, but it's still ticking. What's next?"

"Look for a secondary power source. These bombs usually have a backup."

"Found it," Zack said, spotting the smaller battery nestled beneath a nest of red and blue wires.

"Carefully, Zack. Disconnect that one too." Angela's voice was steady, but there was a note of concern that hadn't been there before.

Zack's hands hovered above the secondary battery, his fingertips brushing against the cold metal. He pinched the connector and gently pulled. Nothing. It wouldn't budge. He tried again, applying more force, but the connector seemed fused to the battery.

"Angela, it's not moving," he said, a hint of strain creeping into his voice. "This setup isn't like the last one. It's different, more advanced."

"Damn it," Angela cursed softly. "They've upped their game. You need to find the motherboard, look for a fail-safe switch."

"Looking," Zack muttered, his eyes scanning the intricate web of electronics. But the design was unlike anything he'd seen before—a labyrinth designed to confound and consume time.

"Angela, there's no switch. No button, no lever. It's like they designed it to be impenetrable." A sliver of doubt wormed its way into his thoughts.

"Zack, listen to me." Angela's voice was firm. "If anyone can figure this out, it's you."

He shook his head, tossing droplets of sweat. "I'm flattered, but I don't think I can. No, I'm gonna have to improvise here."

His fingers curled around the cold metal of the bomb casing, its red digits counting down with unrelenting certainty. He lifted it from the tangle of wires and circuit boards.

"Maya, Riley," he said, "I'm moving out with the payload."

"Okay, Zack," Angela said, her voice low and resigned. "It's your call. But you have to make sure the payload is stable while you move."

Zack nodded, though he knew Angela couldn't see him. He cradled the bomb in his arms, treating it like a newborn. One wrong move, and it was all over.

"Where are you taking it?" Maya asked.

"Still working on that." His eyes darted around the room one last time, and then he waddled out into the hallway.

As he moved down the hallway, he tried to think of the best place to leave the bomb. He wasn't sure of the exact payload it carried, so he needed to do everything he could to minimize its impact.

That was when he saw a sign for the Crypt.

He headed down the staircase, his legs and arms burning with the weight of the bomb.

The Crypt loomed before Zack like the gateway to Hades, the air within heavy with the scent of stone and antiquity. Columns rose like sentinels around the circular space.

Here, beneath the very heart of democracy, Zack faced a trial that could rend it asunder.

"Three minutes," he muttered, glancing at the timer. The bomb, an infernal puzzle box of death, seemed almost to hum with malice in his arms.

"Any luck finding a spot?" Riley asked.

"Working on it," Zack grunted, his gaze sweeping the perimeter. There had to be a niche, a recess, something to mitigate the impact, to shield the world above from the violence he held.

His boots scuffed against the floor as he moved, the bomb's weight a constant reminder of the threat it posed. Then, amid the crypt's sepulchral silence, Zack spotted it—a maintenance hatch near the base of a column, likely leading to a substructure or service tunnel.

"I think I've got something," he said, quickening his pace. "A hatch—it might lead to a lower level, further containment."

"Sounds promising," Maya replied, her tone imbued with a hope that Zack clung to like a lifeline. "Be careful."

As Zack neared the hatch, however, he suddenly spotted movement to his left. A figure stepped out of the shadows, one hand pressed to a bloodstain on his chest, the other hand clutching a pistol.

It was the man he'd shot—the mastermind behind this whole operation.

The man smiled. "Thought I had given up, didn't you? You should've put a few more bullets in me, just to be certain."

"I'll make sure to do that next time," Zack said. He shifted the weight of the bomb in his arms, thinking desperately about what to do.

"I'm afraid there won't be a next time. You and I are going to stay here, just like we are, until that bomb goes off."

Zack's heart pounded within his chest, each beat reminding him of the precious seconds rapidly dwindling, but he kept his gaze steady on the wounded terrorist, his mind kicking into overdrive.

"Two minutes," he said, hoping to trigger some sense of self-preservation in his adversary. "It's not too late to change your mind."

The man just laughed, a cruel sound that echoed through the cavernous space, bouncing off the cold stone walls. "No, I think I am quite content with my decision." His voice was shaky from the blood loss, his gaze slowly glazing over as he kept the gun trained on Zack.

He won't last much longer, Zack thought. *Then again, neither will I.*

"Time's ticking," Zack said, hoping to distract the man as he edged closer to the hatch. "And you're losing more blood by the second. You won't last long enough even to see the fireworks."

"I've made my peace with death, and I know what my death will mean even if I don't get to see the effects. Have you?"

Zack inched closer to the hatch. Right now, if the man fired, there was a good chance the bullet would hit the bomb—which would either cause the bomb to explode or result in a harmless ricochet. But as soon as he set the bomb down, he would be defenseless.

"That's far enough," the man said, his voice hard. "One more step, and I'll put a bullet through your eye."

Zack stopped moving. He sensed the bomb ticking closer to zero, each second a grain of sand slipping through the hourglass. How much time did he have left? Seconds? He had to think of something—and fast.

"Alright," he said. "You win. But if you're going to be a martyr, I think it's only fitting for you to be the one carrying the bomb."

Before the man could react, Zack twisted away and then threw the bomb at him. Caught off-guard, the man instinctively reached out to catch the bomb, which hit his chest and knocked him to the ground, the gun flying from his hand. Zack dived for the weapon, and his fingers had just closed around its cool frame when the man's hand shot out, catching his wrist in a vice-like grip. A battle of strength began, each man pushing against the other's weight. Zack's muscles bunched and strained as he fought to aim the Glock at the man.

Zack grunted, his breath coming in ragged gasps. Sweat trickled down his face, stinging his eyes. His vision blurred with the effort, yet he never lost sight of the man's determined glare.

"You're going to die...one way or the other," the terrorist said through gritted teeth. "So why...make such a fuss?"

Zack threw his elbow, striking the man in the face and causing him to stumble back. "Because unlike you," Zack said as he rose and turned the gun on him, "I have something to live for."

The terrorist sneered, his mouth coated in blood. "Not if I can help it." His hand snaked toward his ankle, drawing a small pistol concealed there. He was not quick enough, however. As the man raised the weapon, Zack fired twice, the bullets hitting him in the chest. His hand fell limp, and he sank back, eyes rolling.

He was finally dead.

Wasting no time, Zack holstered his weapon and grabbed the bomb. His back ached as he dragged the bomb over to the hatch in the floor. His fingers traced the outline of the hatch, seeking the release mechanism. It gave way with a reluctant groan, revealing darkness below—a void that promised oblivion or salvation.

"Here goes nothing," he whispered, lowering the bomb into the gaping maw. As the seconds slipped away, Zack knew that even if this act saved the lives above, the shadows might claim him yet. But he had no other choice.

"Zack, you need to get out of there now!" Riley's urgent voice crackled through the earpiece, slicing through the thick silence of the Capitol Crypt like a knife.

"Leaving the bomb," he said, his breaths harsh in his own ears as he sprinted away from the hatch, leaving behind the device—and the terrorist's lifeless body. The crypt's stone floor, cold and unyielding beneath his boots, seemed to pulse with the countdown timer's relentless beat.

"Move, Zack!" Maya cried. "You don't have much time!"

Despite the circumstances, Zack felt an odd sense of calm amidst the chaos. He had done what he needed to do, regardless of what the consequences might be.

With each stride, the bomb's digital clock ticked away in his mind, a morbid metronome counting down to zero. He willed his legs to push harder, faster. He rounded a corner, barely registering the statues and historic artifacts blurring past. All that mattered was distance—putting as much of it between himself and the bomb before–

The ground lurched violently beneath him as an earth-shattering roar filled the air, the shockwave slamming into his back like a freight train and throwing him forward.

CHAPTER TWENTY FOUR

Zack lay amidst the rubble, mentally checking his body for any signs of serious injury. Dust and debris clung to his hair and clothes. His lungs rebelled against the particulate-laden air, each cough a violent explosion rivaling the concussive force that had hurled him to the ground.

Voices pierced the smoky veil, their echoes bouncing off the shattered remnants of what was once a grand symbol of democracy. Zack's ears rang with a high-pitched whine, the aftermath of the blast that had sent shockwaves through the very foundations of the Capitol Building. He pushed himself up on trembling arms, grit biting into his palms, determination etched into every line of his body.

"Over here!" His voice was ragged, barely audible over the din of sirens and the distant rumble of collapsing masonry. He willed his legs to support him, driven by the innate need to stand tall amid adversity.

Staggering to his feet, he took a halting step forward, then another, his balance uncertain. The smoke curled around him like a living entity, obscuring his vision, threatening to swallow him whole. His eyes stung, tears mingling with the sweat and soot streaking his face.

"Keep talking! We're coming for you!"

Zack's hand went to his earpiece, but it was gone, likely a casualty of the blast that had nearly claimed more than just his equipment. His instincts screamed at him to move, to find a way out, but his training as a government agent held him steady. He knew the rescue team would reach him—his job was just to survive until they did.

The smoke parted like a curtain drawn back by an invisible hand, revealing a squad of firefighters and EMTs, their faces set with grim determination. They approached swiftly, their gear clanking with each step, a symphony of salvation.

"Agent Force?" one of them called out.

"Here," Zack managed to grunt, leaning heavily on a broken column for support.

"Let's get you out of here, sir."

Arms wrapped around him, guiding him away from the epicenter of devastation. Each step was a battle, his limbs rebelling after the adrenaline surge that had fueled his earlier heroics. The cacophony of the rescue operation swirled around him – shouts, the crackling of fire – but within the circle of rescuers, there was a semblance of order, a pocket of calm in the eye of the storm.

As they emerged from the wreckage, the moonlight seemed unnaturally bright. Zack squinted as his head began to throb.

"Easy does it, agent. Watch your step here."

He allowed himself to be led past the threshold of danger and into the open, where medics awaited with stretchers and blankets.

He leaned heavily against the hood of an emergency vehicle, the metal cool through his tattered shirt, trying to piece together the fragments of the past few minutes.

"Zack!"

The urgency in that voice cut through the haze enveloping his mind. Zack lifted his head, squinting as two figures pushed through the throng of medical personnel and uniformed officers. Maya's dark hair was pulled back in a practical ponytail, her FBI badge glinting in the sunlight. Beside her, Riley's presence was a comfort, her determined eyes scanning him from head to toe for injuries.

"I can't believe you're alive," Maya said, reaching him first. Her hands hovered around him as if afraid to touch yet needing to confirm he was real. "We saw the blast...we thought..."

"Is everyone—?" Zack started, but his throat tightened around the words he couldn't finish.

"Alive. Because of you." Relief softened Maya's features. "No fatalities reported, Zack. It's a miracle."

Riley stepped closer, her gaze unwavering. "You did good, partner. You saved lives today."

"Did what I had to do," Zack replied, brushing off the accolade with a shake of his head. His mind darted back to the Crypt: the bomb's weight in his arms, and the sprint for survival.

"You're a hero, Zack," Riley said.

"*We're* heroes," he corrected, locking eyes with her. "We're partners, remember? Couldn't have gotten this far without you."

She nodded, a mixture of pride and camaraderie shining through the soot on her face. They stood there amidst the clamor of rescue efforts, sharing a moment of silent understanding. Their partnership had been forged in the fires of adversity, and today it had held strong when it mattered most.

Zack could feel the weight of his own body beginning to drag him down. The adrenaline that had surged like an electric current through his veins was fading, leaving behind a bone-deep exhaustion. This was the aftermath no one talked about—the leaden limbs, the taste of grit in your mouth, the way your heartbeat seemed too loud in the sudden quiet.

"Let's get you checked out, huh?" Riley suggested, her hand now resting lightly on his shoulder—a lifeline, grounding him.

"Sure," Zack agreed, though his legs protested at the thought of moving again. He was tired, and not just in the physical sense. Battles like these took something from you, chipped away at your resolve, even as they reaffirmed your commitment to the cause.

Before they could find a medic, however, Angela Horowitz appeared, her approach almost spectral through the lingering smoke. "Agent Force," she said, her voice carrying a depth of gratitude that resonated in the stillness. "You've done more than you'll ever know today."

"Ms. Horowitz." Zack nodded to her, noticing the fatigue etched into her features, the strain of recent events. "Just doing my job."

"Your job just prevented another disaster," Angela said earnestly. "Your country owes you a great debt. And not just your country," she added, her gaze solemn and piercing. "People all over the world."

Zack shrugged. He had never cared for praise—besides, it was too easy to give one person credit for the entire team's effort.

"The world's a bit safer tonight because of what we did," he said quietly, feeling a sense of satisfaction begin to replace the exhaustion. "That's what matters."

It was then that Liz Murdock materialized from the throng of emergency personnel, her stride purposeful, her expression somber. "Force," she said, coming to stand beside him, "good work. I imagine you'd like to know who it was you came across inside the building."

"I would indeed," Zack said, bracing himself for whatever came next.

"The man you neutralized," Liz began, her voice low, "was Minho Choi, a known North Korean operative. We suspected their involvement, but now we have confirmation." She paused, allowing the information to sink in. "Choi planted that bomb under direct orders—it's part of a larger strategy to destabilize our nation's infrastructure."

"Choi won't be part of any future strategies," Zack said, the memory of the confrontation flashing before his eyes.

"True, but there are others," Liz warned. "This is bigger than we anticipated, Zack. We need to prepare for what's next."

As Zack fought to hear the director, his ears rang with a high-pitched whine, the aftermath of the explosion still echoing inside his head. The world around him felt muted, like he was trapped under water, every sound muffled and every movement sluggish.

"Zack? Can you hear me?" Maya's voice cut through the fog, her hand on his shoulder grounding him back to reality.

"Maya..." he croaked, his throat raw. "Yeah, I hear you."

"Sit down before you fall down," she insisted, her tone brokering no argument.

He acquiesced, his legs folding beneath him more from necessity than obedience.

"You need to rest, Zack," Riley said. "You've earned it."

"Rest," he repeated, the word foreign on his lips. It seemed an impossible luxury given what had just transpired.

As he sat, every ache and pain announced itself. There was a throbbing in his left side where debris had pelted him, and his fingers were numb, likely from gripping the bomb with all his might. He glanced down at his hands – his father's hands, strong and calloused from years of military service – and realized they were shaking.

"Shock setting in," he murmured to himself, recognizing the signs. "Adrenaline crash."

His eyes wandered over the damage: the blackened walls, the fractured ceiling. Lives had been saved today, yet the weight of responsibility bore down on him with relentless gravity. How many more Minho Chois were out there, plotting destruction in the shadows? How many more times would he throw himself into the fire?

"Hey," Maya said softly, bringing his attention back. She offered him a bottle of water, which he took with gratitude. The cool liquid was soothing, a small mercy amidst the chaos.

"Thanks," he managed to say, offering her a nod. Her concern was a balm to his battered spirit.

"Just relax," she said, her hand resting lightly on his arm. "We'll take it from here."

"Only for a moment," he murmured, allowing his eyelids to droop shut. Just for a moment, he'd let the darkness claim him, before rising again to stand watch over the home he vowed to defend.

And before he knew it, he was asleep.

EPILOGUE

The morning sun had begun its ascent, casting a gentle glow over the rows of somber headstones as Zack Force stood silently at one such grave, the grass still wet with dew beneath his boots. His shadow stretched long and thin across the manicured lawn of the cemetery, reaching out like an intangible connection to the past.

"Hey, Dad," Zack whispered, his voice scarcely more than a rumble against the quietude. "We did it. We stopped them."

With hands that bore the weight of last night's violence — the tremors now stilled — he reached into his jacket pocket and pulled out a weathered military challenge coin. The insignia of his father's unit was etched upon it, a tangible piece of legacy. He placed it delicately atop the cool granite of Douglas Force's headstone, letting his fingertips linger on the metal, as if transferring what remained of yesterday's adrenaline into this symbol of honor.

"Hope you'd be proud," Zack continued, his gaze tracing the engraved letters of his father's name. "Just wish you could see what we're up against now. It's a different battlefield, but the same fight."

As he straightened, Zack's muscles protested, a symphony of aches singing through him, reminders of his frantic race through the Capitol Building Crypt, the bomb's weight in his arms.

His phone vibrated in his pocket, a jarring intrusion into the moment. Pulling it out, Zack saw Maya's name flash on the screen. A smile cracked the hard lines of his face—a rarity reserved for those who'd earned his trust.

Just checking in on you, the text read. *Hope you're holding up alright.*

Zack paused, his thumb hovering over the keyboard. Maya Walsh. She'd been a revelation, her intuition sharp as a sniper's aim. Together, they'd formed an unexpected partnership, her insights complementing his own relentless drive.

Survived worse, he typed back, then hesitated. He wasn't usually a sentimental guy, but sometimes he made exceptions. *Thanks for everything. Couldn't have done it without you.*

The pleasure was all mine, she wrote back. *If you need a hand again, you know how to reach me.*

Zack smiled, thinking, *I just might do that.*

* * *

Zack turned the key in the lock, ready for a long, relaxed day free of responsibilities. He had no idea how he would spend the day, which was precisely what he needed—a day without plans, without crises.

A blank canvas.

He pushed the door open, bracing himself for solitude, only to be met by a wave of sound and warmth that nearly knocked him back. His home, usually a quiet refuge, thrummed with life.

"Surprise!" echoed as bodies moved from shadow to light, revealing familiar faces: Riley Carter with her unwavering smile, Maya Walsh whose eyes sparkled with shared secrets, Director Murdock standing tall, and a handful of other friends and colleagues.

"Wha—" Zack started, taken aback.

"Come on, Zack," Liz called out, stepping forward with a grin. "You didn't think we'd let you brood in peace after all that, did you?"

Riley approached, her eyes scanning him with that familiar intensity. "No good deed goes unpunished," she said with a wink.

She leaned close and whispered, "Oh, and if you're ever that reckless again, I'll make sure to kill you myself."

Same old Riley, Zack thought.

As the sounds of laughter and clinking glasses filled the room, Zack's gaze found Maya. She nodded slightly, an unspoken understanding passing between them. He cleared his throat, trying to find words that seemed lost in the din of celebration.

"Speech! Speech!" the chant began, playful yet insistent.

Swallowing the lump in his throat, Zack stepped into the makeshift spotlight, the faces around him blurring into a tapestry of camaraderie. "I'm not one for speeches," he began, his voice steady despite the tremor in his hands. "But last night—last night showed us what we're capable of when we stand together."

He paused, collecting his thoughts. Unity. Perseverance. They were more than words—they were the lifeline that had pulled them through the impossible. "We were up against the wall. Outnumbered. Outgunned. But we had something they didn't—a bond that doesn't break under pressure. We have each other's backs, and that," he lifted his gaze, meeting the eyes of his comrades, "that is why we succeeded."

A swell of agreement rippled through the room, affirming his sentiment. "This victory, it's not about me. It's about us. Every piece of information gathered, every lead followed, every sacrifice made—it was a collective effort."

He paused, gathering his words. "Protecting our country, our people, isn't a one-man job. It's a relentless pursuit that we embark on together." Zack's chest swelled with pride. "And if we continue to stand united, there's nothing we can't overcome."

Cheers erupted, filling the space with a resonance that seemed to chase away the shadows of yesterday's terror. Glasses rose in salute, and for a moment, Zack allowed himself to bask in the warmth of their shared triumph, the success not just of thwarting a disaster, but of forging a family bound by duty and honor.

As the applause died down, Zack caught Riley's eye. She gave him a subtle nod, affirming their unbreakable partnership. Looking around at his team, his friends, Zack knew that whatever threats lay ahead, they would face them together. And with that knowledge came a sense of resolute peace amidst the lingering echoes of war.

The room settled into a comfortable murmur. Zack's gaze fell on Maya again as she talked with an old veteran, the light from the vintage chandelier casting a warm glow on her face, reflecting the determination and tenacity that Zack had come to admire so much. She broke away from her conversation and clinked her glass softly, drawing the attention of the room.

"Zack," she began, her voice steady but laced with emotion, "if anyone deserves to be honored tonight, it's you." The guests turned their focus toward her, glasses paused mid-air, conversations halted.

"Last night—you know, I've never seen anything quite like it." Her eyes met Zack's, holding them with a depth of understanding that only those who have walked through fire could share. "Running into danger when everyone else is running away—that's not just bravery; that's a calling."

Silence draped over the room as Maya continued. "You see, what Zack did wasn't for glory, it was because he knows the value of life, of freedom. He feels it in his bones—the weight of duty, the importance of safeguarding the innocent."

She lifted her glass higher, a beacon in their midst. "To Zack Force, who embodies the spirit of the unsung heroes—those who protect, serve, and sacrifice without expecting anything in return. To the man who, despite his own wounds, stands ever vigilant, unyielding in his resolve to keep our nation safe."

The room erupted in cheers, a chorus of admiration and respect. Zack felt a lump form in his throat as he locked eyes with Maya once again. A bond forged in the crucible of shared tribulation—a steadfast alliance that went beyond words. He gave her a nod, the simplest gesture of gratitude, but one laden with profound acknowledgment.

"Thank you, Maya," Zack said, his throat suddenly dry. "Your words mean more than you know."

As conversations started up around the room, Zack began drifting between groups of friends and colleagues, each exchange punctuated by handshakes and pats on the back. But within him, a tide of contemplation ebbed and flowed, a silent undercurrent beneath the surface cheer.

He'd been through hell and back, nearly giving his life along the way. His body still ached from the ordeal, a constant reminder of how close he'd come to being a name on a memorial wall.

He paused at the window, studying the cityscape beyond. It was out there, somewhere beyond sight: the next danger that would rise up to threaten his country.

A sense of clarity gripped him then, the realization that this celebration was but a brief respite in an ongoing war—a war not fought on distant shores, but here, within the very heart of his homeland. And he was one of its sentinels, standing guard against the insidious tide that sought to erode the pillars of liberty and justice.

Zack let his gaze drift back to his friends: to Riley, Liz, and yes, Maya. They were more than comrades; they were his shield-bearers, his fellow warriors in the ceaseless battle for righteousness. Together, they'd weathered storms and stared down death's grim visage, emerging stronger, more united.

When the call came again, as it inevitably would, Zack Force would answer it. For his father, for his country, for all that he held dear—he would stand ready to stop the darkness and bring dawn to the land he swore to defend.

Warmed by these thoughts and the alcohol coursing through his body, Zack scanned the room and found himself staring into Liz's eyes. She was in the hallway, her phone pressed to the side of her face, looking deathly pale.

Zack set aside his glass and strode toward her, reaching her just as she finished the call.

"Everything alright?" he asked.

She took a shaky breath. "No, not really. A government lab in Seattle was just attacked."

Zack took a moment to absorb this news. "What were they after?"

"A deadly pathogen." Liz swallowed hard and looked him square in the eye. "One that could wipe our race off the face of the earth."

NOW AVAILABLE!

PATRIOT DOWN
(A Zack Force Action Thriller—Book 2)

When top scientists are kidnapped and a deadly pathogen stolen, Homeland Agent Zack Force plunges into the heart of danger to thwart a devastating attack. Can he decipher the clues from this radical new threat before the final countdown?

PATRIOT DOWN (A Zack Force Action Thriller—Book 2) is the second novel in a new series by thriller author Vin Strong. The series begins with PATRIOT FORCE (book #1).

Zack Force is an action thriller you won't be able to put down. With heart-pounding suspense and unforgettable twists, this series will have you falling in love with a brand-new action hero—and turning pages late into the night. Fans of Vince Flynn, Tom Clancy, and Brad Thor are sure to fall in love with their next favorite action hero.

Future books in the series are also available!

Vin Strong

Vin Strong is the author of the BRIANNA DAGGER spy thriller series, comprising five books (and counting), and of the ZACK FORCE thriller series, comprising five books (and counting).

An avid reader and lifelong fan of the thriller genres, Vin loves to hear from you, so please feel free to visit vinstrongauthor.com to learn more and stay in touch.

BOOKS BY VIN STRONG

ZACK FORCE THRILLER SERIES
PATRIOT FORCE (Book #1)
PATRIOT DOWN (Book #2)
PATRIOT RISING (Book #3)
PATRIOT STRIKE (Book #4)
PATRIOT TARGET (Book #5)

BRIANNA DAGGER THRILLER SERIES
MAZE OF SPIES (Book #1)
MAZE OF TRAITORS (Book #2)
MAZE OF LIES (Book #3)
MAZE OF SHADOWS (Book #4)
MAZE OF SECRETS (Book #5)

Made in the USA
Monee, IL
18 April 2024

57141458R00085